The Adventures
of
Alonzo Woodchuck

THE ADVENTURES OF ALONZO WOODCHUCK

Robert Ellis Klein

Illustrations by S.E. Carey

BAYEUX

First published in 1994
by Bayeux Arts, Incorporated,
Suite 240, 4411 Sixteenth Avenue, N.W.,
Calgary, Alberta T3B 0M3, Canada

Canadian Cataloguing in Publication Data

Klein, Robert E. (Robert Ellis), 1947-
The adventures of Alonzo Woodchuck

ISBN 1-896209-08-4

I. Title
PZ7.K53Ad 1994   j813'.54   C94-910424-8

Printed and bound in Canada at
Friesen Printers, Altona, Manitoba

The Adventures of Alonzo Woodchuck is dedicated to Ruth and Ernest Hermann who have supported me in this effort from the moment that Alonzo first wandered into my garden.

Acknowledgments

I would like to thank my wife, Charlotte, who has somehow put up with me for twenty-something years and who inspired me to take the camp letters to our two sons, Jonathan and Michael, and transform them into this story.

I am grateful to Jonathan who spread the letters throughout the camp and reported back reactions to the exploits of Alonzo and Andre.

Thanks to Michael who provided major editorial support through his keen sense of the use of language.

I am very appreciative of the support that my parents, Herbert and Semah Klein, have provided to me.

Finally, a special debt of gratitude is due to Andre, our cat, who volunteered much of the material for this fantastic adventure during our frequent early morning chats over breakfast.

Chapter 1

Alonzo Woodchuck was the youngest child of Cassandra and Monte Woodchuck. He was born after the last cold snap of Spring and spent his early days huddled in the burrow with his brother and sisters. Alonzo also spent a great amount of time with his mother, because his father was always out and about making deals for vegetables and other goodies. Whenever his father came back, he would always tell the family of his adventures in the woods and around the vegetable garden of the big house. Alonzo was fascinated by these bold tales and he was most eager to be out of the burrow so that he could see all of this for himself.

In late May, Alonzo was finally permitted to venture out on his own. Up to this point, his parents had taken him on short jaunts about the woods and had taken him near the edge of the deep grass from where he could see the human creatures in their garden. He could also see the big burrow where the humans lived, and this excited him no end.

Before leaving the burrow that morning he combed his reddish brown fur, brushed his teeth carefully and had a quick nibble on some very nice corn cobs that his father had traded with an unsuspecting squirrel for a half-rotted butternut squash. Alonzo then went to the low brush behind the big burrow. He watched carefully to see if the human creatures were about. When he did not see any of them he stood on his hind legs in order to get a good sniff and also to look over the tall grass toward the vegetable garden. No one was around and it seemed safe to venture closer. Alonzo Woodchuck boldly headed for territory where no woodchuck had ever gone before.

Lying in the deep grass by the edge of the garden, Alonzo Woodchuck looked toward the big house and saw the human creatures seated in some kind of a large machine moving backwards from the inside of the house. The machine turned away from him and went down a long, wide path and then he lost sight of it. All he heard was the sound of the engine fading in the distance. Then there was silence once more.

Woodchuck burrows are rather crude. They have dirt walls, dirt floors and although they have several chambers, they are not very roomy. The burrows are cool in the summer, cool in the fall, and downright cold in the winter and spring. The woodchuck sleeps during the winter months on the floor of the burrow, where there is nothing to keep him warm other than the fat and fur of his body. Considering the general discomfort of it all, Alonzo was eager to see what the human burrow was like. As he came out from behind the big rock and slowly made his way towards the big house, he kept hoping that all of the creatures had gone away in the large machine.

In making his way through the bushes and along the edge of the lawn in the direction of the big house, Alonzo moved very slowly. He did not want to be seen. In the event that there was anyone still remaining in the human burrow, he knew he had to be very careful in his movements.

There was no stopping now as he dashed across the lawn to the safety of the space under the stairs leading to the deck and a large screened-in porch. He lay very still by one of the posts which was supporting the porch. With his heart beating very quickly and his fur standing up straight on his back, he almost forgot to breathe.

Lying there, he realized that he had no plan on how to get into the big house. How did the human creatures get in? He looked around and took note of what he could see from his hiding place. Under the porch there was a large grey wall and in the middle of the wall was a window through which he could see right into the big house. Suddenly, he stopped. The noises he heard were not the thumpety-thump of his rapidly beating heart. They were coming from within the big house and they sounded just like human voices. Alonzo, not sure what to do, was terrified at the thought that there were still people inside. He had come so far and did not want to go back to the woods. It would mean giving up his chance to learn about this big house.

Alonzo Woodchuck took in a big gulp of air and swallowed. It made a little noise that startled him, but he was determined to go on and not turn back. Shaking a bit, he crawled slowly towards the window under the porch. At the very edge, he raised his head so that he could just peer into the house. If any of the creatures were in there he could hopefully make his escape before they discovered him.

Alonzo's attention was immediately drawn to a large box that appeared to be across the chamber. On the front of the box, he saw several creatures just like those which he had seen earlier. They were talking and moving around, but they seemed to stay in the box and did not leave. He watched the humans who were much smaller than the creatures he had seen leaving the big house, and who had the ability to change size and have their heads take up the entire front of the box. The television was certainly very strange indeed.

Watching and listening for some time, he wondered whether the creatures were watching him as well, so he lay perfectly still.

Without warning, the window moved and struck him right in the nose. Alonzo ducked down and the outwardly opening window passed right over his body. Too terrified to move, he worried that he had been discovered. What horrible fate would befall him? With his paws outstretched, he tried to cover himself with the dirt and grass around him. His little heart was now pounding so loudly he barely heard the new noise coming from the edge of the window opening. Slowly raising his eyes without moving his head, he peered right into the eyes of a strange new animal. It was a creature more like him, than a human. Behind its large glowing yellow eyes, it had black fur, and a spot of white on its face.

"Hey, woodchuck, what are you looking at, huh?" Alonzo did not move. He couldn't. Again the creature spoke "What is it that you think that you are doing out there? No wood to chuck, huh, is that it? I mean really, man, what is your problem? Cat got your tongue?" Alonzo remained frozen in his spot. And with that this black fur-covered creature began to laugh loudly and spoke again.

"You are boring me man, you really are. Look, let me set your mind at ease; I was more or less just interested in making your acquaintance. As I am sure you can appreciate, some days are more boring than others and this is one of them. So why don't you stop lying there like some blithering idiot and come in. Let's have a nice friendly chat? Whadya say?"

Alonzo frumpled his brow a bit realizing that maybe this was not the end for him. After all, this creature was rather pleasant in an annoying sort of way. But cautiously Alonzo still continued to lie still thinking of what to do next while keeping his eyes on the creature.

Dropping his head right into Alonzo's face the creature again spoke: "Oh, alright, have it your way. Just lay there scared silly that I am going to eat you or make you into a fur hat and I will just continue my conversation with myself here. " Alonzo did not relax.

"Listen pal, this is getting rather silly. I'm talking and you're staring at me like you are amazed that I am even speaking to you. What? Am I being rude and not formally introducing myself, is that the problem? Well, excuse me! Let's not stand on ceremony then. I am Andre. And who are you, Mr. Woodchuck? I mean what do your fellow woodchuckians call you? Woody? Chuck? Chuckie-baby? Well?"

As Alonzo continued to stare, Andre now shook his head in disbelief. "Was danger all in his mind?" Alonzo thought. Maybe this creature was friendly though his tone seemed rather rude.

"Look, are you coming in or not? At this point I need some amusement, so don't bother telling me who you are, but come in before every 'skeeter within twenty miles flies in here looking for its next meal. So, are you in or are you out? Just get on with it, man." Andre gestured with his paw for Alonzo to get up and come into the big house through the window, stepping to the side as if to show Alonzo exactly what he had in mind.

Andre moved away from the window, hopped into the bathroom sink and down onto the floor, while Alonzo picked his head up to peer through the window, watching Andre's every move with great care. Alonzo's mouth was open in complete amazement. Andre chuckled to himself as he wandered over to the television screen which was now exhibiting a female body- building competition. Settling himself down on the couch, he pretended to watch while keeping an eye and ear out for his invited guest.

Alonzo came to his feet, but kept his eyes locked on the couch where he had last observed Andre, though he could not see him now. The scenes from the big box intrigued him enough to take a very deep breath, put his front paws over the window and stick his head inside the room. To Alonzo the bathroom was just a chamber with some very odd looking stuff in it. He poked his nose into the air and took a few exploratory sniffs to ensure that it was safe to enter. Deciding to cast all caution to the wind, he hopped into the sink, jumped down onto the floor, and slowly made his way over to the couch where Andre was reclining.

"Ah, look what the cat dragged in," Andre said , laughing again over his clever play on words. "Come on over and sit here and tell me your life story. I've got five minutes before the start of my soap opera.

Alonzo was sitting up on his hind legs mesmer- ized by the images which had changed to two new creatures. One was just like Andre and the other was like the humans he had seen earlier. The Andre-like creature had his head in a bowl and the human was nodding its head and showing its teeth in a pleasant fashion.

"That stuff tastes like dried mud! I can't believe

any self-respecting cat would eat that garbage!" Andre commented. "Hey kid, why not have a seat up here and take a load off your feet? There is no need to be so weird, I'll explain it all to you in due time," he chuckled.

The bewildered woodchuck looked over at the cat who had dark coverings over his eyes that seemed to stretch from his ears. His left paw was in a bowl, drawing out some white and yellow puffy stuff that he put into his mouth and chewed loudly. "Hungry, buddy?" the cat inquired. "The microwave popcorn isn't bad, not bad at all, low in salt. Come up here for crying out loud and I'll let you have a pawful. You must be hungry; I'm always hungry."

It was true that Alonzo was a bit hungry, but being in a state of shock, he found it increasingly difficult to sort all of this out. Andre let the sun-

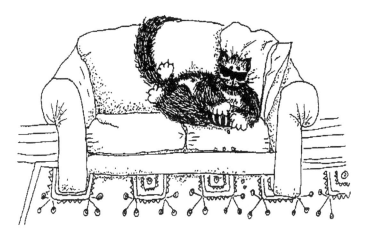

glasses drop to the end of his nose and he peered over the top of the frames at the confused woodchuck staring at him.

"Gee whiz kid, were you born yesterday or what? Let's get with the program, pal. Up here!" he said , patting the couch with his paw. "It's OK when the people aren't here. You would be amazed at the kind of stuff I do, really." Alonzo's eyes began to widen.

Andre stuffed another pawful of popcorn into his mouth and then reached down and turned off the television with the remote control. The screen which Alonzo had been watching went black. "There," said Andre, "now we shall have each other's complete attention. So I gather that this is all very new to you and of course you have a zillion questions, right? Just fire away. Andre has all the answers, all of them!"

Because of a huge lump in his throat, Alonzo had not uttered even the slightest grunt. Instead, he looked over at Andre and showed a rather silly grin. Andre, in turn, flipped his shades back over his eyes and looked up at the ceiling in exasperation. Clearing his throat, Alonzo startled both of them. "Ah, um, nice burrow you got here, yeah," Alonzo ventured.

"Oh that's beautiful," retorted Andre, "I've invited quite the conversationalist I see. Listen woodchuck, this is not a burrow, it happens to be a contem-porary-styled single family dwelling."

"Its Alonzo, not Woodchuck."

"Who's not a woodchuck? I read, and I know a woodchuck when I see one or perhaps smell one, ha, ha! What are you talking about?"

"No, no, Alonzo, that's my name. Not Wood-chuck, Alonzo!"

"Yeah," bellowed Andre laughing, "and what do your friends call you, Al or Zo, eh?"

"Alonzo, just Alonzo," said the woodchuck in a matter-of-fact way.

" Well, now we are getting somewhere. I was just about to turn on the tube and watch some wres-tling to keep from falling asleep. Thank goodness! So, Al, what do you want to do?"

"Alonzo!"

"Ok, Alonzo," Andre agreed, "What did you have in mind? A little Nintendo or ping pong perhaps? I am in the mood for a game of something. Or maybe, given your obviously perplexed state, you would prefer to learn the facts of life from the "Master" eh, Al?"

"Excuse me . It's Alonzo! Alonzo, Alonzo!" said a frustrated Alonzo.

"Whatever you say , Al. Whatever you say."

Chapter 2

"Come on, there's no one else here but the two of us. I'll give you the tour," Andre shouted, his voice trailing away as he bounded up the stairs to the first landing and disappeared from Alonzo's view. "Hey, are you coming up or what?"

Alonzo had moved towards the first set of stairs and was alternately peering upward and sniffing. This burrow was much bigger than he had imagined. It seemed to reach well beyond the height of any tree he had seen. Everything seemed so big. He could hear the patter of his guide's feet on the floor above, but he was too scared to see if the human creatures were really gone. Moving closer to the first stair, he looked up at Andre on the second set of stairs, returning his look downward with a very condescending stare. Alonzo smiled rather sheepishly and slowly started up the staircase to the first landing.

"Look, Chuckie, I don't have all day to wait, you know. I have a very busy schedule and frankly, I had not planned on your being here and all. So would you please move a little faster so we can get on with it? Is that too much to ask, eh? " complained Andre.

Mustering up some false courage, Alonzo said, his voice cracking, "I'm coming, I'm coming. Ah, um, are you sure there is no one here except us, I mean...."

"Do you see anyone, Chuckie? Do you?"

"Well, no, but they could be hiding and this could all be a trick and, and...."

Andre moved away from the top of the stairs and sat back to lick himself as if to show the woodchuck his complete confidence in having the situation under control. He briefly looked up and there was Alonzo, his mouth open, looking about the first landing and about to embark onto the second set of stairs. Moving to the edge of the stairs, Andre called down to the timid woodchuck: "Hurry up will you? I have some terrific stuff to show you up here. It will knock your socks off man, knock 'em right off!" The woodchuck looked down at his feet. He wasn't wearing socks.

Alonzo made it up the first set of stairs and now he was standing on some kind of very smooth, flat rock. His feet felt cool as he moved about and looked around. There was a huge door and a window that looked out from the human burrow onto the front yard and street. He had only heard about this from his mother's warnings of the dangers of the big house. Looking out of the window for just a minute, he could see a number of other big human burrows. He stepped away and turned to the second set of stairs covered with a soft grey short-clipped 'grass'. At the top, a very annoyed Andre stood waiting for him.

As Alonzo finally began the ascent to the second level, Andre turned and walked into a big chamber directly opposite the top of the stairs. Slowly making his way to the top, Alonzo lost sight again of his host and so moved quicker so that he would not become lost in this very strange place.

At the top of the stairs he stopped. Standing on his hind legs, which is something that woodchucks instinctively do when they want to either take a deep breath or check things out carefully, he let his eyes wander all around him. To his left was a very large chamber with a stone wall climbing clearly to the roof. At the bottom of the wall was an opening and pieces of a tree neatly stacked next to it. There were several couches like the one below and another set of

14

stairs leading up even higher. There were other large structures in the room that he had never seen before. As his eyes came forward again, there was Andre sitting in the middle of the big chamber high off the floor on some kind of a wide, flat wooden stump. Andre was smiling and watching Alonzo. Around the wooden stump was a shiny wet-looking grey area. Andre was sitting on an island in the middle of what seemed to Alonzo to be a little pond.

"Hey pal, "Andre called, "come on up here."

"I don't feel like swimming," said Alonzo, in response to the invitation.

"What?" the cat said. "Swimming? It's a tile floor man. Where have you been hiding all your life, in the woods or what? My goodness, this is going to be a lot of work."

The little woodchuck looked away and smiled briefly, mostly out of embarrassment. This entire matter was becoming more than he thought he could handle in one day. He then moved towards the floor from the short carpet that was on this level too. He timidly stuck his front paw onto the floor and was pleased that it was hard and did not feel wet. "It was probably frozen," Alonzo thought. He had heard about what happened to water in the winter, but of course , woodchucks slept during the winter so no one had ever really verified this. He could not wait to report that water freezes in the summer in the human burrows! He stepped forward again, not completely sure that it would support his weight, then stopped and looked around. This time he did not get on his hind legs but turned his head from side to side to investigate. "Man, will you move it? What's your problem, haven't you ever been in a kitchen before? Come on up here! Hop onto that stool and then climb onto the top of the counter," Andre said, staring down at the timid woodchuck who was now looking at him with his mouth wide open. There were four stools which looked like very small couches with tall legs. Alonzo, now with both feet on the tile walked around under these stools, sniffing them and pushing them ever so slightly with his front paws. Andre meanwhile, was pacing the top of the stump, looking very tired.

The cat lay down on the counter top and surveyed Alonzo, who was now on his hind legs figuring out how to get onto the stool seat. "Woodie, I am beginning to wonder why I 'm even bothering to do this for you. If I didn't feel that you needed to be educated, I would have left you outside with the rest of your stone-aged friends. This is the future man; let's get with the program. Up! Up! Get up onto the stool and it's no sweat to the top, really. For crying out loud, do it. NOW!!!" yelled Andre, to the overly

cautious woodchuck.

Alonzo made it to the seat of the stool on the energy generated from his fear of what the cat might do if he delayed any longer. From the stool it was just a small hop and he was on top of the counter where he stood perfectly still and looked around by moving just his head. He wasn't sure how steady he was, still being very close to the edge.

"Come on, give me some paw, man, give me some paw! Well done, Woodie-baby, Aw right!" exclaimed a smiling Andre.

The woodchuck did not move. Andre reached over and grabbed his paw and struck it with his, whereupon Alonzo jumped back and almost lost his balance. He looked at the cat in a startled but once again curious manner. "This is going to be a long day," said Andre shaking his head, " a very long day indeed."

Alonzo lowered his head and for the first time since accepting the cat's invitation his fear and excitement were replaced by a new emotion. He wanted to cry. Humility and sensitivity were not Andre's strongest character traits; however, he was not totally devoid of them either. Watching the woodchuck shaking and sniffling with a big tear rolling down his snout finally moved Andre. He handed Alonzo a handkerchief and gave him a little pat on the back and walked to the edge of the counter facing the dining room. Alonzo wiped his nose and his eyes and turned to see the cat with his back to him. He noisily cleared his throat, but Andre did not move. Now more confident that the counter would not tip over, Alonzo walked over to sit next to the cat. He handed Andre back his handkerchief.

"You know that there is one really big dog living at that house over there," said the cat, pointing at the huge human burrow which could be seen through the dining room window. "You've got to watch out for them, Woodie, er, ah, I mean, Alonzo. You have got to watch out for them!" Alonzo looked up at Andre and the cat gave him a little smile.

Chapter 3

Alonzo Woodchuck and Andre, his new friend and teacher, sat together on the island in the kitchen in silence for several minutes before Andre turned to Alonzo and said, "Hungry? Boy, I sure am! So, what's your pleasure?"

Andre jumped down from the island and headed for a large box standing just at the entrance of the kitchen chamber. The box had a very glossy black front and Alonzo could see not only a woodchuck who strongly resembled himself staring at him, but also a cat who looked just like Andre walking towards the box. Alonzo blinked and then looked again, concentrating on the other woodchuck, who, like Alonzo, had not moved. Alonzo moved his paw and the other woodchuck moved his paw. He stood up on his hind legs and glared at the other woodchuck, who did the same thing. Just then the box swung open and there was a bright light showing lots of things inside. "Why did the other woodchuck disappear from view?" wondered a bewildered Alonzo.

Standing at the door of the refrigerator, Andre called to Alonzo, who was looking at all of the curious things inside. "See anything that you like, little guy? There is a ton of stuff in here, eh? I think I might have some cold pizza and a little tossed salad. And you?

The woodchuck tried to pretend he knew exactly what a pizza or a salad was. "Er, ah, I'll have what you are having, of course!"

"Well, that makes it very easy doesn't it?" said a happy Andre, as he reached in and took out an object wrapped in a silver paper-like material. With his other paw he grabbed a small white dish with a bright red cover, putting them on the floor, and closing the door. He asked Alonzo one more question: "What do you want to drink? Water? Milk? Grape juice? We got 'em all!"

Alonzo, dumbfounded, smiled and shrugged his shoulders; it was all he could do. Andre smiled and said, "Look, you can have some of what I am going to have, OK? The grape juice will be perfect with the pizza, but you have to promise not to spill it because if it stains I'll get into all kinds of trouble. The humans who share this place with me think that I just eat the cat food they drop into my bowl each morning or the occasional leftover they so generously throw my way. But when they are gone or when it is late at night, well, buddy, I have whatever I want. They never miss it and if they do, they just blame one another. It's pretty funny actually. As long as I clean up and leave pieces of cat food scattered around my bowl, they keep from getting suspicious. So, is it grape juice you want?"

Alonzo nodded, but without any idea what Andre had just babbled about. He was more concerned with climbing down from the top of the counter to join the cat on the floor. Perhaps the best way down was to trace the way he had come up. Moving to the edge backwards, he got down on his belly and pushed his back legs out from the counter, and down toward the seat of the stool. Unable to reach, he pushed back on his belly a little more. Below him Andre was humming and moving the food across the floor. Alonzo's feet were just not long enough and he knew it, so he took a deep breath, closed his eyes and pushed extra hard with his front paws while wiggling his hind paws downward.

It all happened so fast. His belly slid too far on the counter, his feet hit the top of the seat and the stool rocked backward. He fell forward, eyes closed, toward the floor and toward Andre who was carrying the pizza, the salad, and the grape juice. There was a huge crash and Andre yelled something that Alonzo had never heard before.

Lying on the floor with his eyes still tightly shut, Alonzo felt a sweet smelling wetness over the back of his body and feet. He could also feel the struggling cat trying to push him off and heard him mumbling under his breath. The woodchuck opened his eyes and took a very quick look about. The stool was lying on the floor near the entry. The container with the grape juice that stains was on its side and the dark purple liquid was all over him, Andre and the floor. The bowl with the salad no longer had a top and there were greens, tomatoes, carrots and cucumbers scattered all over the place. Alonzo turned his head and found himself staring straight into Andre's face. The cat was glaring at the woodchuck. Alonzo smiled for lack of anything else to do. Andre failed to see the humor of the situation and lost control.

"You idiot!" screamed Andre, "Look at this mess. Ugh! The grape juice is all over the floor and it stains, man, it stains. Get off of me for crying out loud, get up!" With that the cat pushed Alonzo with such force that the woodchuck found himself skidding through grape juice and salad across the floor on his back while watching the ceiling fly by. The

wet, grape juice-covered woodchuck came to rest against the bottom of the refrigerator door. Andre was not pleased, standing in a puddle of salad and juice. Alonzo started to speak, feeling he had to say something.

"Button it, Woody. Don't you say a word or you will be someone's winter hat." Andre was standing on his hind legs and his front paws were on his hips. The white tips of all four of his paws were a deep purple and little bits of salad were stuck to his fur. He continued to glare at the woodchuck. Today was certainly no longer boring. He surveyed the floor, fur standing on edge as he examined the damage. Andre closed his eyes and counted to one hundred forty by sevens, which is like counting to twenty by ones. While he did this, he brushed the salad from his fur and licked his paws.

When he had finished counting, he took a deep breath and shook his head. Much calmer now, he spoke to Alonzo in a controlled manner, thus insuring the poor woodchuck's life. Alonzo was still lying on his back in the puddle of juice and peering at Andre over his little belly. He had a very silly, dumbfounded expression on his face. "Don't just lie there man, get up and help me clean this place. We will be in real trouble if the humans come home and see this. Come on, let's get moving."

Alonzo struggled to his feet to find a dry spot on the floor. Now, most animals shake themselves in order to get dry. The woodchuck was no exception. He stood there on his little spot and tilted his head to begin shaking. Out of the corner of his eye, however, he saw the cat about to scream. "Don't you dare shake or you will be the latest in cat cuisine!" finished Andre.

The woodchuck did not move. Andre sloshed over and pulled a cloth from the oven door located just over Alonzo's head and handed it to him. "Use this to wipe off the juice," said a calmer Andre. Looking puzzled Alonzo squinted a bit at the cat. Andre shook his head, and gave out a big sigh as he rubbed the woodchuck's body with the towel he had now taken back. At last the cat realized that he was not dealing with the world's most sophisticated woodchuck.

After drying himself, Andre looked at Alonzo and asked: "Well buddy, got any ideas about how we ought to clean this up, huh?" Before Alonzo could come up with the likely suggestion, of eating and slurping it all up, Andre was bounding out of the kitchen and down the hall to the left. The woodchuck carefully went to the doorway looking after the speedy cat.

"No problem little guy. We'll use the vacuum,"

he yelled back, as he opened the closet door in the hallway.

Alonzo thought that sounded like a splendid idea since he had no idea what a vacuum was or what a vacuum did he watched as the cat went into the closet. Hearing a large crash and stepping back to the wall for protection, he cautiously peered down the hall. There was Andre , dragging a large black hose toward him.

"Woodie? Whoops, I mean Alonzo, could you please give me a hand with this? Wait! Hold it, don't forget to wipe your feet! If we get grape juice on the rug, it will be the end of us for sure," said Andre, just as Alonzo was about to run into the hallway onto the carpet. Eager to help his friend, he had not even given a thought to his wet and purple feet. Alonzo took the towel from the leg of the fallen stool and wiped all of his paws until they were dry. He was now ready to help Andre with the vacuum.

Alonzo, walked with Andre back to the closet, which was a tiny tall chamber. Inside was a tall silver-type pipe connected to a black box-like object which rested on the floor. The two animals dragged the vacuum down the hall to the hose.

Andre stared at the hose and then stared at the thing that they had brought to it. Alonzo stood next to the confident cat and waited for something to happen. The cat did not move. "Ah, you know how this works right, kid?" he asked to Alonzo, who did not move and quizzically turned his head to the stumped cat.

"That's great, just swell," the cat bellowed. "I should have paid more attention when the 'what-did-you-break-this-week-cleaning-lady' was here." "Hmmm. I think that you put this in here," he muttered, "and then this must go into the wall over there." Andre was carrying one end of the black hose to a small, covered hole at the end of the hall in the wall. After putting the hose down, he walked back to check the box and the other attached end, and stood in front of it to push on the hose with his paws.

Feeling that he was not being terribly helpful, Alonzo made his way to the end of the hose, lifted it up and with what he thought was a brilliant stroke, pushed it into the plate in the wall. Suddenly a huge

whirring sound rushed into the hall. Alonzo heard a loud cry from the cat. The hose had somehow grabbed Andre's tail and he was yelling and screaming at Alonzo, who watched Andre move very close to the box at a rapid rate. Then there was a loud thump as the box and the cat attached to the box struck the wall. With all four paws out in front of him, and with his tail disappearing in the box, Andre let out a wild: "YEEEOWWWW!" Alonzo froze. With his nostrils flared and his eyes wide open, Andre screamed again, "Pull the hose out, pull it OUT!" Alonzo wrinkled his brow and looked at the wall and then at the cat and then at the wall again. "PULL IT OUT, NOW!" the cat pleaded again. The terrified woodchuck moved as quickly as woodchucks can move and pulled the hose from the wall plate. The noise stopped.

Andre lay belly down on the floor. He was panting and sweat was pouring from his forehead. Slowly he tried to stand and pull himself away from the vacuum. He looked at Alonzo who was shivering uncontrollably. Andre, shaking his head very slowly, walked down the hall and past the woodchuck. At the entryway of the kitchen he turned to Alonzo and said: "So, how long do you think it will take us to eat the salad and slurp up the grape juice?"

Chapter 4

The woodchuck and the cat were lying on the floor of the kitchen, their heads propped up against the wall, rubbing their tummies. Andre let out a big belch and turned to the woodchuck who was asleep. "Not a bad meal, eh kid?" he said.

Alonzo woke with a start and looked over at the cat lying on the floor. Andre slowly shook his head and got to his feet. He looked around the kitchen which they had cleaned up, or eaten up most of the mess. The only remaining evidence of their folly was a rolled-up ball of tin foil which had covered the pizza slices. The floor was a bit sticky, however, and the cat pondered the situation.

" We have to clean this floor, man. The humans will know something is up when their feet stick to it," he said to Alonzo, who had no idea what he was talking about. The woodchuck was now standing next to the cat and sniffing about. When he took his first step he realized there was indeed a problem. The floor was very sticky.

It reminded him of the day he stepped in the pitch on the pine log and ended up dragging into the bur-row loose grass and twigs. His mother was furious as she had just swept out the chambers and was admiring her work before her youngest son showed up with half the woods stuck to his paws. That was not a pleasant time for Alonzo as it took him several hours to remove the grass and twigs and pitch from his feet. It took him several more hours to recover from the pain on his rear end from his mother's broom. Now he stood perfectly still, listening intently to any suggestion that Andre might have that could save them both from what Alonzo thought would be certain misery.

"We'll need to wash it and when we are done no one will know that there was a problem," the cat declared with a sense of satisfaction. "And after we wash it then we will wax it and make it shiny." Andre smiled at Alonzo. Alonzo had no idea what waxing was, but he thought that washing the floor was a terrific idea if it kept him from getting things stuck to his feet. He didn't want things sticking, and he sure was not interested in explaining any of this to his mother.

Andre was opening a wooden door that was about his size near the window that looked out towards the garden. The woodchuck had often seen the human creatures standing and looking out of this window while playing with water and dishes. The wooden cabinet under the sink was now wide open and the cat was examining its contents. There were a number of bottles with blue and green water in them. There were small colorful rectangular things with holes partially through them and some boxes with pictures of humans on them. Andre took several of the colorful rectangular things out of the cabinet and put them on the floor. He then took out a red bucket with a handle on it and eyed the top of the counter. Andre quickly leaped to the counter, disappeared into the sink, and began to make a strange noise. It sounded like rushing water, just like when he would go down to the brook early in the morning for a drink.

"Throw up the pail would you?" Andre implored. There was the cat standing on the counter motioning towards the bucket and pointing to the water running now from a silver pipe. Alonzo obliged. Andre filled the bucket and handed it down to the woodchuck, turned off the water and dropped to the floor .

"Alonzo, I had better do this myself, but you can help me wax it when the water dries," Andre stated. "Are you into ice skating?" The cat was again confusing him. Obviously he did not realize that woodchucks hibernate all winter and have therefore never had the opportunity to experience winter sports.

Andre motioned for Alonzo to stand in the corner away from where the juice had been. The cat then put the colorful rectangular things in the bucket of water, got them very wet and removed them, squeezing the excess water back into the bucket. He then proceeded to rub the floor with them. He put them back in the bucket and repeated the process until he had done all of the floor which had been covered with grape juice. Alonzo watched this interesting process and stood smiling at the cat who was wringing out the last sponge into the bucket.

"Now the fun begins kid. Now we are going to do some serious skating and you, my friend, are going to love it," Andre said with a huge smile on his face. He put the sponges on the floor and pushed the bucket towards Alonzo; he then climbed onto the island and opened a drawer just below the counter, reaching into the drawer and poking about for a minute or two. He looked up at the woodchuck and raised his eyebrows and widened his eyes. Reaching in he then threw a clump of stringy-brown circles which fell to the floor. Andre closed the drawer and walked across the island to one of the stools which he used to make his descent to the floor a bit easier.

Alonzo began checking out the stringy things and sniffing them while Andre dragged over two of the sponges and stood on them with his back paws. He reached over and took two of the stringy things and wrapped them around both his paws and the sponges. Standing erect, he took a few short steps to make sure that the sponges were securely on his paws. The woodchuck wondered what the cat had planned.

"Here, stand on these and I'll wrap the rubber

bands onto your feet. That way the sponges won't come off while you are skating," the cat explained. The cat lifted his feet and slopping and sloshing his way to the cabinet, he removed a tall bottle with a red cap. He unscrewed the cap and poured some of the contents onto the floor, stepping onto the liquid with his sponged feet and spinning himself around. The cat nodded to Alonzo and stepped away from the puddle. Andre pointed his nose high into the air, held up his front paws in an outstretched manner and then with his right hind paw gliding forward, he lifted his left rear paw and pointed it behind him. The cat seemed to be floating as he passed Alonzo. He then switched feet and glided around the far corner of the island, out of the amazed woodchuck's view.

When Andre reappeared his front paws were behind him resting on his back. Head down and looking ahead, he gained speed and Alonzo's mouth fell open while the cat passed him again on his way around the corner, and again a second time. This time he had his back to the woodchuck and he turned and stopped right in front of Alonzo. "Your turn, big guy," said the cat, removing his sponge skates from his paws. "But we need some music. Wait here."

The woodchuck wasn't going anywhere. Andre took off and bounded from the kitchen through the dining room and into the chamber Alonzo had first seen at the top of the stairs. Alonzo looked around the corner and spotted the cat opening a cabinet with a see-through door and noticed some stange objects visible through it. Andre moved his paw along an object in the cabinet and suddenly there were loud pleasing sounds. Andre stood back from the cabinet and moved his head to the side a few times keeping time with the beat. Alonzo found himself swaying a bit also, but he dared not take any steps with his sponge skates.

Andre came back to where the woodchuck was standing and strapped on his skates again. He then glided over to the bottle and poured some more wax onto the floor. "Al, come over here and put some wax on those things," he demanded. Alonzo struggled with the awkward sponge skates and made his way to the puddle of liquid on the tile.

"Step into the wax and then move your feet around so that the sponge soaks the stuff up," instructed Andre. "Then do as I do and, believe me, it will be one of your life's biggest pleasures!"

Alonzo followed the advice of his friend and let the sponge skates soak up the wax while Andre poured some more on the floor and stood in it until his skates had plenty of wax on them too. "Watch me now," the cat called over the sound of the music, "and do exactly what I do."

Again, Andre got into position and propelled himself gracefully across the kitchen floor. He disappeared once more around the island. As he came into view he motioned for the woodchuck to follow. Alonzo moved very slowly, still very unsure of himself. Copying the cat, he held his nose high in the air, spread his arms out and pushed off with his left rear paw while lifting his right. Andre,who was doing spins on one leg, watched intently as his student took a first glide.

Unfortunately the woodchuck had given himself too much of a push. Soon Alonzo realized that he was out of control. His front paws began waving about and his right leg was swinging wildly and he was heading right for the cat. Alonzo knew that there was no way that he could stop. Andre, who had glanced away for a second, turned and saw too late that the woodchuck was hurtling towards him. Their bodies met in an explosion and collision of fur and slammed into the cabinet. Bouncing from there, they slid quickly across the floor into the bucket of water. The impact of their bodies striking the bucket caused Andre to flip high in the air. Struggling with his paws flailing about, he landed head first in the bucket of water. The splash from the cat spilled water all over the woodchuck.

Alonzo had both eyes closed. Lying on his stomach, he opened one eye and looked in the direction of the red bucket. He observed two front paws gripping the top rim of the bucket and saw the cat's head slowly rise. Andre's eyes were wild with frustration. Alonzo did not move as the entire head of the cat appeared and a small stream of water came from Andre's mouth as he opened it to speak. Alonzo instinctively covered his ears with his paws but it hardly lessened the piercing scream of the drenched and furious cat.

Chapter 5

Tired of these misadventures resulting in humilia-
tion and embarrassment, Andre realized his lessons to
the young woodchuck were not going well at all. He
looked over at Alonzo. The woodchuck was too
frightened to move and needed to be calmed. The
skating adventure was over and fortunately the
cleanup would be easier this time.

"Alonzo, my man, what do you say we take a
tour of the rest of this place? I promised you I would
knock your socks off and I mean to deliver!" said the
cat. "Seriously man, there is a lot more to see and a
whole lot more to do."

Alonzo was afraid of this. He had seen and heard
so many new things, he was not sure that he was
ready for more adventure. But few woodchucks had
ever spent this much time in a human burrow, of that
he was sure. He took a deep breath, smiled at the cat
who was now sponging up the spilled water into the
bucket and said, "Well, I guess that I can stay a bit
longer. When are the humans coming back to their
burrow?"

The cat was now rubbing a towel all over his
body in an effort to dry himself off. He stood on his
rear paws and with his head tilted to one side, tried to

get some water out of his ear with the end of the towel. Alonzo was very curious as to how he did this, as woodchucks just counted to ten and shook. "Don't worry Al," answered Andre, "we have plenty of time. The humans will be gone for the rest of the day."

Alonzo was only half listening as he was still trying to understand about losing socks that he did not seem to have. Just as he was about to ask the cat about the socks (although he knew it was risky to ask too many questions of the cat), Andre bounded out of the kitchen and headed down the hall to the left. Alonzo had no choice but to follow.

Opposite the door to the closet which stored the vacuum was another chamber. Alonzo, who hurried to the doorway so as not to lose track of the cat, watched as Andre entered this room. The woodchuck followed him. Andre was up on another huge stump-like object in the corner of the room, which looked like the cabinets in the kitchen except that it had a short stool in front of it which Andre had used to jump to it. On the very top were several things that the woodchuck had never seen before. The cat seemed very comfortable and turned to beckon Alonzo to climb up onto the small stool and then onto the top of the desk. He followed the cat's suggestion and as he was almost onto the flat surface, he noticed that Andre was punching a small black rectangular box with his paw. Alonzo could hear beeping sounds coming from the box as the cat continued to strike it.

Alonzo noticed a black curled string at the side of the box which was attached to an even stranger object that looked like a black bone. The sounds seemed to be coming from the top of the bone-like thing. Andre had now finished dialing the phone and he picked up the receiver, holding it to his ear and to his mouth. Alonzo's mouth as it frequently had done that day, opened once again and he stared at the cat with the telephone in his paw.

"I'm calling for Chinese food," he whispered to Alonzo as he held one paw over the bottom of the

receiver. "I was getting hungry again and I figured that we could take a drive and go get it. Don't worry, we'll bring it back and eat it here."

Andre turned and spoke into the receiver. He seemed to lower his voice and so the woodchuck assumed that this was what you did when you used a telephone. Andre, however, knew that he had to disguise his voice or the person on the phone would immediately know that it was a cat ordering and not a human. "Yes, good afternoon. I would like to place an order to go."

"To go where?" wondered Alonzo.

"We'll have an order of fried shrimp, some spare ribs and a vegetable dish for the woodchuck, er ah, I mean for Chuck," said Andre, quickly nodding to Alonzo. "What? Oh yes, we'll pick it up in about ten minutes. Great! The name? Ahhh, it's Alonzo, yes, Alonzo Wood." With that the cat hung up the phone and turned to the woodchuck. The cat knew that he had to explain it all to Alonzo, but he also knew that they did not have a lot of time either.

"Al, ole pal, I have ordered us some terrific food from a restaurant about two miles from here. We have to drive over and pick it up. I promise you that it will be the best meal that you have ever had. Really it will be much better than the pizza. Trust me!"

The woodchuck did not understand much the cat had said except the last part. Trust was not something he was prepared for, given what had happened already. But he was curious and he needed to know if this had anything to do with socks.

Andre jumped down from the desk and took off down the hall. Alonzo slowly climbed down from the chair and went to look for the cat. The cat was standing in one of the other chambers in the human burrow in front of a closet filled with human clothes.

"We'll need to wear some clothes so that the humans at the restaurant do not suspect anything," he said. "Is there anything special that you would like to wear?"

Alonzo walked in, stood next to the cat and looked into the closet. "So this is what humans do to cover their skin," he thought. "I wonder what happened to their fur?" He had often watched the human creatures and had been very interested in the different furs they had. Now he was even more amazed to see that they had so many. He looked down at his own fur and thought that it would be very exciting to change it and try on the human creatures' clothing. He peered intently into the closet as the cat moved

forward and pulled several garments out.

Andre held up a yellow shirt to the chest of the
woodchuck. He looked at it carefully, and then shook
his head, letting the shirt drop to the floor at Alonzo's
feet. Alonzo looked down at it. He liked the color
and was about to bend over and pick it up when
Andre shoved a brilliant bright blue shirt in front of
him. The cat was smiling. The woodchuck looked at
it and he too thought that it was very nice.

"This is definitely you, kid," the cat said as he
admired his choice.

"Do you think so?" said Alonzo, overcome with
excitement about wearing human-creature fur.

"Yes, absolutely, but you are going to need a hat. I mean, as soon as those humans see that face and those ears, they are gonna know that something is up." Andre dropped the other garments onto the floor, reached into the closet and pulled out a ski hat with lots of reds and greens in it.

"Here, put this on," said Andre as he pulled it over Alonzo's head, covering his ears. "Put on the shirt too."

The cat helped the woodchuck pull the shirt over his hat-covered head. This all felt very strange to Alonzo, but he was pleased. After all, now he could have a different colored fur, different from all the other woodchucks. He wanted desperately to take this outfit back to his burrow to show his brothers and sister. They would probably want clothes too. Andre was now moving him around. As he turned, he looked up and found himself staring at a woodchuck dressed in the same clothes, even stranger was a cat standing with him that looked just like Andre.

Alonzo turned quickly, remembering his experience with the strange woodchuck he had seen in the kitchen earlier. Andre sensed his confusion and started to laugh. The woodchuck had never seen a mirror before.

"That's us buddy," the cat said turning back to the glass leaning against the wall. "See?" he asked, as he waved his paw at the two animals in the glass.

The woodchuck squinted his eyes and moved a paw just as the woodchuck in the glass did the same. He shook his head and so did the other woodchuck. He looked again and realized that he was staring at himself.

"We don't have time for this!" the cat bellowed. "We have got to get going or they will give our stuff away."

Andre raced about looking for something. He opened a drawer on the table next to the bed and took out a black piece of leather that was folded in half. The woodchuck could see some green sticking out from between the folds. The cat put the black leather thing on the floor and stood in front of the closet. He scratched his head with one paw and then reached in and took out a red-hooded sweatshirt with the word Montreal written in white letters across the front. He then picked up the wallet and put it into the pocket on the front of the sweatshirt.

"Let's move it, man. We are way behind schedule here."

Andre darted out of the room, headed down the hall and down the stairs. Alonzo quickly followed, but not before taking one more good look into the mirror at the woodchuck wearing the shirt and ski hat.

Chapter 6

At the bottom of the stairs, Andre was adjusting his sunglasses and impatiently waiting for the woodchuck having some difficulty negotiating the stairs. The shirt was big on him and a couple of times he stepped on it and nearly fell. He decided, after almost tumbling down the first flight of stairs, to back down the second set. This was a very slow process. As he turned to check his position, he could see the cat wearing the sweatshirt and sunglasses, standing impatiently with his front paws on his hips.

"Move it, Al! I can just about taste those ribs and there is nothing worse than cold Chinese food."

"I am doing the best I can," said the cautious woodchuck. With that he tried to hurry and as he

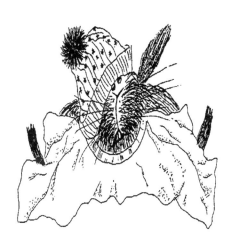 extended his back paw, it caught on the edge of the shirt and down the stairs he went. Alonzo landed in a heap at the feet of the cat. Andre looked down at him, shook his

head and then turned to open the big door behind him.

Alonzo picked himself up and gathered the bottom of the shirt in his paws. The ski hat had slipped down over one eye and he had to stop and adjust it so he could see. The woodchuck was feeling very warm and there was perspiration running down his forehead. "Wearing clothes makes you very hot," he thought. Nevertheless, he followed the cat through the big door.

When he had gone through the door, Alonzo looked up and saw a very large silver-colored thing. It looked a lot like the thing that he had seen the human creatures leave the burrow in earlier. Andre was opening a door to the thing and was getting inside. The woodchuck looked around the big chamber where the silver thing was. It was huge. At the opposite end were two of the biggest doors he had ever seen. Next to the silver thing was a big space which must have been the resting place of the thing he had seen earlier. Suddenly, Alonzo heard a big groan and the huge door behind the silver thing in which the cat was now seated began to open. The woodchuck stood in the open doorway and just began to shake.

"Alonzo!" screamed Andre, "Close the door to the house! We don't want the cat to get out, now do we? Get in! Get into the car, will you please?"

The cat leaned over to the other side of the car, and the door on that side opened. The woodchuck simply stood there, and Andre dropped his sunglasses to the end of his nose. Peering over them, he motioned to the animal in the shirt and ski hat to get in.

First, the woodchuck went back to the door to the house and closed it. He then walked very carefully to the car, not really sure of what might happen. At the door of the car he stopped and looked in. The cat was seated across from him, behind a large circle-like thing. Andre had both paws on the steering wheel and his feet were outstretched in front of him. The cat had re-adjusted his sunglasses and turned to the woodchuck.

"Get in and close the door, Woodie. I feel the need for speed."

Alonzo climbed into the car and sat in the big seat in the same manner as the cat. He moved his rear end around and was surprised at how comfortable it was. He looked over at Andre and smiled.

"Wonderful," said the cat, "now close the door and put on your seatbelt." Andre was pointing to the black strap that came over his shoulder and across his belly. Alonzo reached out and pulled the door shut. He then reached over his right shoulder and pulled on the black strap. At first he did not pull it far enough and he was unable to get it over his body.

The strap brushed against the ski hat and both eyes were covered. Andre let out a big sigh and reached over to help his passenger. Alonzo pushed the ski hat back up onto his forehead while the cat pulled the black strap over the woodchuck's shoulder and clipped it into the piece by the edge of the seat. Alonzo nodded his appreciation and the cat once again just shook his head.

"Are you ready to put the pedal to the metal?" the cat inquired.

Alonzo said nothing. Andre then grabbed the circle thing with one paw and with the other he turned a silver and black thing that was sticking out of the circle. The little woodchuck jumped but the black strap held him down as he heard the sound of the engine starting. He was terribly frightened. Looking over at the cat however, he felt a little bit more re-laxed. Andre seemed to have everything under con-trol and was actually smiling. The cat looked over at Alonzo and reached for the stick which was standing straight up between them. He grabbed it and pulled it back until the woodchuck heard a click.

"Relax, kid, this is going to be great fun!" Alonzo had heard those words of confidence all too many times. He gripped the sides of his seat very tightly, took a deep breath and closed his eyes. The car slowly backed out of the garage.

Chapter 7

When the car had pulled entirely out of the garage, the cat turned to the woodchuck and said, "Close the garage door, will you please?"

Alonzo looked at Andre, who was now moving the stick between them further back with one paw. The other paw was on the circle thing. The woodchuck tried to get out from under the strap and was going to open the door of the car.

"No, no, silly! See that black thing over your head?" asked the cat. "Reach up and push the white button, the door will close by itself."

The woodchuck did not even question the cat. He merely did as he was told and the door started downward to close. It was now becoming very clear to Alonzo that animals that lived with human creatures knew an awful lot.

The woodchuck had been taught about the animals of the woods by his parents. He knew which ones were very bright and which ones you could sneak up behind without their knowing you were even nearby. But this cat was certainly the cleverest animal in and out of the forest. He was sure that he was the first woodchuck ever to operate an electric garage door opener, let alone ride in a car.

Andre, pleased that the door was closed, reached up and adjusted the rearview mirror. Alonzo watched his every move and this amused the smug cat. The car moved down the hill of the driveway and almost came to a complete stop at the bottom. Andre looked first to the left and then to the right. Then he pulled the steering wheel to the left. The car started to move slowly out of the driveway and onto the street. Alonzo looked out of the window behind the cat and watched as the house got smaller. He suddenly realized that he could no longer see the woods or the big rock near his burrow. He wondered if he would ever see them again.

"Beats walking, doesn't it?" asked the cat. He looked over at the woodchuck staring out the window. Sensing that Alonzo was both excited and also very frightened, the cat reached over and patted the woodchuck on the shoulder. Alonzo did not move, but continued to look longingly out of the window back toward the house and the woods.

Andre reached for the radio and turned it on.

Music filled the interior of the car. The cat looked over at the woodchuck and saw him move just a little to the sound of the music. "Aw right!" he said, tapping the steering wheel with his paw. Alonzo smiled. He was enjoying this adventure, so far.

The cat turned his attention to the road ahead. He slowed the car down as he came to an intersection and brought the car to a stop. Again he looked both ways. Another car was coming and Andre waited for it to pass. Then he turned and pulled the car to the right onto the new street. The woodchuck was no longer looking backward, but now was looking out of the window next to him at all the human burrows that lined the street.

After a short while, Andre spoke. "I suppose you are wondering how I learned to drive."

The thought had certainly crossed the woodchuck's mind, but given the events of the day, nothing surprised him.

Andre continued. "Usually when the people go for a ride and take me along, they make me ride in this awful cat box. They think I am comfortable in it and that I actually like riding in the darn thing. Well, I don't. But it pays to be observant. At first I used to complain and whine. They did not care. So then I decided to watch what they did. I mean, I live with some fairly weird people and I figured that if they could operate this thing, then so could I."

Alonzo was paying more attention to exactly what the cat was doing. The car was going faster now and outside the window the burrows and the trees were whizzing by.

"So when they go out," the cat continued, "I take this thing for a spin. You have to admit that I am pretty good getting out of the garage and all, eh? I mean for the first time on the street, how am I doing?"

The little woodchuck was incredulous. "Had he said, 'for the first time on the street'?" he thought, turning his head slowly away from the window towards Andre.

Andre smiled. "Well, if you can pull out of a garage and drive up and down a driveway, then the street is no sweat!"

Alonzo swallowed very hard and turned his eyes to the front of the car. His paws gripped the seat and his knuckles turned white. Alonzo could see other cars moving by quickly. There seemed to be no end to them.

Andre slowed the car and brought it to a stop. He looked over at the woodchuck. "Hey, man, relax. Everything is cool," said Andre. But for Alonzo, this experience was more than he could handle. The woodchuck was sweating profusely. He did not move.

"Want me to roll down the window?" the cat asked. "It will be cooler. My, you look terrible."

The woodchuck with the shirt, the ski hat and the very white knuckles, did not even look at the cat, but merely nodded. Andre reached to his left and with his paw pushed a button. The window next to Alonzo started to slide downward and almost immediately he felt the cool air rush in. It made him feel a little bit better, but then when he looked up he could see all those cars in front of him speeding by. He took another big gulp and swallowed.

The cat strained to look to the left and the right. The line of traffic was continuous. They seemed to sit there for a long time. Just when things seemed clear on the left, there would be a long line of cars on the right. Andre was getting impatient. Alonzo was just grateful that he was still alive. He wondered why he had been so curious about the human burrow. Things had been a lot simpler in the woods.

Suddenly, a car behind them wanted to cross the intersection. Andre turned and looked over his right shoulder at the huge car to the rear. It was very close and all he could see was the front of the hood and the headlights. The driver of the big car was in some kind of a hurry. He beeped his horn loudly several times, at which Andre again turned and looked over his shoulder. The cat then turned his gaze to the horrified woodchuck.

"It's now or never, Woodie!" he shouted. With that the car lurched forward and shot through the intersection. Alonzo's eyes had been riveted to the road ahead across the busy street. As the car rocketed forward he closed them tight. All he could sense were the incredibly loud sounds of screeching rubber and colliding, crunching metal.

The woodchuck opened one eye and turned his head toward the driver. Andre was holding the steering wheel tightly. The cat shot a glance at his passenger. "Hey buddy, was that neat or what? We made it!"

Alonzo opened the other eye and looked back over his left as the car sped away. Behind them were two or three cars all crumpled together and some human creatures waving angrily at them with their fists shaking in the air.

Chapter 8

Andre seemed to be quite relieved that they had passed the intersection and had made it across. Alonzo was still shaking from the experience. Andre appeared to be very relaxed, meowing to the music coming from the radio. The woodchuck tried to enjoy the ride and once again looked out of the window. The window was down and the cool breeze made him feel much better.

"What's that noise? Do you hear that?" asked Andre with a sense of urgency and concern.

"I don't hear anything," said Alonzo, "except the music from over there." The woodchuck was pointing at the lighted dial from the radio.

"No, it's not coming from the radio. I have heard that sound before, but I just can't seem to place it," the cat replied.

Now Alonzo's ears perked up. Woodchucks have excellent hearing. He had not heard it as clearly before because the ski hat covered his ears, and the wind rushing through the window made it difficult to hear. It was a very high pitched sound, almost like the sounds birds in the woods make when they warn others of danger.

WHOOP, WHOOOOP, WHIRRRRRR. The sound was getting louder and closer. The cat was looking around inside the car, trying to figure out where it could possibly be coming from. He hoped nothing was broken, as he knew he would have a very hard time explaining it to the humans. WHOOP, WHOOOOP, WHIRRRRR,WHOOP, WHOOOOP, WHIRRRRRR!

Alonzo was looking about wildly. This noise seemed to be almost on top of them. His eyes were now wild with excitement. His little woodchuck heart was pounding almost as loudly as the sound that kept getting closer. WHOOP, WHOOOOP, WHIRRRRR, WHOOP, WHOOOOP, WHIRRRRR, WHOOP,WHOOOOP,WHIRRRRR.

Suddenly a flash of white light exploded in the car, causing both the cat and the woodchuck to blink. Then a flash of blue and another flash of blue. The two animals looked at each other. The flashes of light, white and blue, filled the interior of the car. Andre gripped the wheel and Alonzo once again gripped the seat until his knuckles were white.

Andre looked up and his eyes caught the rearview mirror. All he could see were the flashing headlights of a huge car and on its roof he saw the bar of blue lights blinking rapidly on and off. He began to slow the car and pull to the right.

"Ah Woodie, we have a little problem here, but, but , I, I, can handle this. Trust me," the cat explained.

"Trust me?" Alonzo thought. The woodchuck was now beginning to get the idea that this cat did not have all the answers. As the car stopped by the side of the road, Alonzo pulled his ski hat down to the top of his eyes and turned to look out the window. He couldn't bring himself to look at the cat sitting behind the wheel. Andre adjusted his sunglasses and pulled tight on the strings to the hood of the sweatshirt.

"Good afternoon, boys!" said the huge police officer, his voice booming. All Alonzo could see was the top of the blue pants of policeman. On one side was a huge black leather case of some kind with a

silver thing sticking out. On the other side, were two
silver circles linked together with a short chain. In
the middle, was a huge silver buckle. The cat was
staring right at the buckle. Slowly the body of the
policeman moved backward. His over-sized hands
came up from his sides and his big, fat, fingers
gripped the bottom of the open window. His enor-
mous stomach and chest were now visible and Alonzo
could see the bright shiny badge on his shirt. He bent
down more and his large, round, and rather red face
filled the opening of the window.

"Well, out for a leisurely drive today, fellas?" he
said with a half smile. "Let me see your license and
registration, kid."

Andre was now looking right into the mirrored
sunglasses of one of the biggest human creatures he

had ever seen. The sound of his booming voice had made his ears ring with pain. The cat tried to speak. He could not. Instead he smiled and began to fumble through the pocket in the front of the sweatshirt for the wallet he had brought with him. Alonzo had almost fainted as he saw the huge face. As Andre reached into the sweatshirt pocket with his right paw and removed the wallet, he swung his elbow upward, slamming shut the wide open jaw of the woodchuck.

"It is a lovely day, isn't it, officer?" the cat finally responded, lowering his voice as he had done on the phone when ordering the Chinese food. "I am sure I have what you want in my wallet here ." The cat had watched a lot of television and had seen this type of thing lots of times before. In most of those cases the human creatures had given the policeman some cards or papers. After the policeman looked at them he would say something and then there would be a commercial. Andre, knowing a commercial was coming would leave the room in order to be the first to get a snack or a drink and so he would miss what actually happened on the show. This same, clever cat really had no idea what a license or a registration was.

Looking into the wallet, the cat grabbed the first piece of paper he saw and smiling, handed it through the window to the officer. The officer stepped back and examined the paper carefully.

"Congratulations. Apparently you passed beginner swimmer, but I really need your license," said the policeman with a slight, but menacing smile.

"Oh, of course, ossifer, er, ah,.... I mean, officer, my license. I am sure it must be here somewhere. Ah, what color is it?" Andre asked.

The officer bent down closer to the window and put his gorilla-like face right up to Andre's. "What color is it?" he bellowed, causing Andre to roll his head backwards and the woodchuck to grip his seat even tighter. The officer's breath smelled like horrible tobacco product and the stench filled the car.

Andre, gasping for fresh air, again fumbled through the wallet. There were lots of cards and papers. It had not occurred to him that the human who owned the wallet was too young to have a license. Then he remembered something he had heard in one of the television shows to which he had actually paid attention.

"It must be in my other pants," he replied. "Yah, that's it. When I got dressed this morning, I must have left my license in my other pants. Yah, they're in my other pants." Alonzo looked over at the cat. He was not wearing pants, just the red sweatshirt.

"I am afraid that you have been watching too

much T.V., son," the policeman said, stepping back from the window as he tried to center his rather large belly behind his belt buckle. "Where are you two going, eh?"

"Well, officer," said the cat, now gaining confidence in his ability to handle this little problem, "we were hungry and we were on our way to pick up a Chinese food order. Care to join us, sir?"

The officer stepped back further and eyed the two creatures seated in the automobile. He took off his hat, looked skyward for a second, wiped the sweat from his forehead with his sleeve and then just shook his head. "All right, all right. But just try to be careful that you bring your license with you whenever you drive. By the way, what are your names?" he asked taking a pad and pencil from the pocket of his uniform pants.

The cat was stunned. "Ah, er, its Andre, Andre Katz and this is my buddy, Al, Al Wood," he finally blurted out. "Al, say hello to the officer, huh?" Alonzo leaned towards the window and gave the policeman a little nod with his head.

The officer made a few notes and looked at the two animals very carefully. With a perplexed look on his face he said, " Are you two from around here? I thought I knew most of the kids on these streets, but I don't remember you two."

"Ah, we go to private school, sir, and we are just home for the weekend," said Andre, speaking now with incredible confidence.

"Oh, it must be one of those Florida schools," the officer responded. Nodding at Alonzo he went on, "Your buddy has an incredible tan! "

Andre smiled.

"One other thing, kid, " the officer said as he walked back towards the police car with the flashing headlights and the blinking blue bar light, "wear shoes or sneakers, not just socks, when you are driving, ok?"

"Yes sir, officer!" Andre shouted, looking down at his bare white paws. Alonzo looked too.

Chapter 9

The white police car pulled out from behind their car and headed down the road. Alonzo and Andre watched the car and as it passed each of them waved to the officer. He waved back. Then the two creatures looked at each other. "Wow, that was really close, eh Al?" said Andre, feeling rather pleased with himself.

"What just happened?" asked Alonzo. "Who was that human creature?"

"Look kid, just forget it. Everything is ok. We just had a temporary setback. I don't know about you, but I am famished. I can smell that Chinese food now."

This cat had gotten them out of every jam so far but the woodchuck was a very long way from home. He had no idea what Chinese food was, but he did feel rather hungry, especially with all that had taken place.

Andre restarted the car and after looking to the left and into the rearview mirror, he pulled forward. He drove somewhat slower and that made Alonzo more comfortable. "Relax man, enjoy the ride. How about those tunes?" the cat asked, trying to reassure his friend that the worst was over. Alonzo was looking out the window and wondering about what might possibly happen next.

The car turned down several streets and at each intersection the cat was able to manuever the car flawlessly. No police cars stopped them and no other angry motorists raised their fists at them. The music was pleasant and occasionally the two animals would look at each other and smile. Andre was even beginning to like his new companion. Alonzo was having similar positive thoughts about Andre, except that he was now sure that this cat didn't know everything.

"There it is!" shouted Andre, as the car came to a stop. Alonzo looked forward but all he saw were several cars in front of him and a huge yellow thing hanging in the sky with three eyes. The top eye was a bright red. "Over there," said Andre, pointing to the left. "Hoy Toy Chinese Food To Go". Alonzo looked and there to the left was a big sign with lots of

writing on it and a picture of a little man holding two sticks and a bowl of something.

When the cars ahead started to move, the woodchuck looked up and saw that the big yellow thing now had closed its red eye and had its green eye open. The cat drove through the intersection and turned to the left behind one of the other cars.

Andre steered the car into the parking lot of the Hoy Toy Chinese Food To Go Restaurant. He drove between two white lines on the ground and came to a stop. He pushed the stick in between them to the top and turned the silver and black thing on the steering column. There was silence. The music had stopped.
Alonzo looked at Andre. The cat was fumbling with the leather wallet he had put back into the pocket of his sweatshirt.

"Here take this in, give it to the man behind the counter and he'll give you our order," he told Alonzo, thrusting a small green and white paper at him.
"Don't forget, the order is under the name of Wood, Al Wood."

The little woodchuck did not move. He had the general idea. Andre wanted him to get the food and give a human creature the green and white paper. Alonzo looked over at the impatient cat and shook his head. "I am not going in there. You do it," he told Andre.

"Wait just a minute here, ole buddy. I mean like, who called the restaurant and ordered the food? Who drove the car all the way here? Who fast-talked that police officer into not giving us a ticket? We are a bit ungrateful, are we not?" the cat responded.

"But I have never done anything like this before. I can't talk to a human creature. They'll know right away I am a woodchuck as soon as I speak," whined Alonzo.

"Nonsense! You can do it. I'll tell you what to say." said Andre, trying to sound convincing. "By the way, there will be change from the money I have given you. Don't drop it."

The cat reached over and unclipped the woodchuck's seat belt. Alonzo did not budge. Instead he held onto the sides of the seat very tightly. The cat stuffed the money into his left front paw which was practically glued to the seat. "Come on kid, get out and go in and just ask for the order for Wood. There is nothing to worry about. The human creature will never suspect anything if you do exactly as I tell you."

"Well, if you are so sure that it is so easy, then maybe you should do it. After all, you are the one with all the experience in things like this," said Alonzo, as he loosened his grip and pushed the twenty dollar bill towards the cat. "I mean, I could watch you and perhaps do it just like you next time."

Andre thought for a moment. He was certainly surprised at the logic of the woodchuck, who up until now had done just about every thing he had asked him to do. He decided to try a different approach. "Well, if that's the way you want to do things, Alonzo, that's ok with me," he calmly responded. "But, I kind of saw us as a team, you know? Two buddies, for life, going around and having great adventures. Always being there for each other. Willing to go that extra mile." The cat got very emotional as he spoke.

As Andre continued, Alonzo began to believe that this was important. It was a test, a test of their friendship. The cat stole a look at the woodchuck to see if his plan was working. Alonzo had his head buried in his paws. He was feeling very sorry that he had given the cat such a hard time.

Alonzo looked up. Andre turned away just as he did. "OK! I'll do it!" the woodchuck cried. "Just tell me what to say."

"Nah, you don't really have to, after all, I mean," said Andre, playing it for all it was worth.

"No, I will. It's my duty as your friend," Alonzo yelled.

"Look, all you do is go in there and when the man behind the counter asks you what you want, you tell him that you are there to pick up the Wood order. He'll give you a bag with the food and you give him the money. Then he will give you some change which you will take and after thanking him, you leave."

Alonzo was trying his best to listen carefully and hoped that he could remember everything that Andre said. He kept nodding his head, but he really was very confused. For the sake of their friendship, however, he felt he could no longer wait. The woodchuck reached for the door handle and opened the door.

"Wait!" Andre screamed, "Tuck your tail into the bottom of the shirt and pull your hat over your ears, ok?"

As the door swung open, the woodchuck hopped down from the seat. WIth the door blocking the view of anyone nearby, he stuffed his tail into the back of the shirt so it could not be seen. Then he fixed his hat and looked to the cat for approval. Andre nodded and Alonzo took a deep breath and headed for the front door of the restaurant. It was the longest walk he had ever taken. His little heart pounded inside of his body.

He had a small amount of trouble opening the big door at the entrance, but was fortunate that some human creatures were just leaving and they pushed as he pulled. He tried not to look at them, but he could

68

sense that they were staring and he thought he heard one of them make a comment about his being a very short person. As the door swung closed, he looked back and saw the cat sitting in the car watching him. He waved a small wave with his paw, but the cat, not wanting to attract too much attention, pretended not to notice.

Alonzo walked over to the counter. It was very high and he could not see if anyone was there if he stood too close to it. Also, no one could see Alonzo either. He stepped back. Suddenly a big round face appeared at the top of the counter and looked him right in the eyes.

"Prease, can help you?" said the man, looking down at the little woodchuck in the shirt and ski hat.

"Huh?" said Alonzo, rumpling his forehead, as he tried to act naturally.

"Prease, I take your order rittle boy?" the man asked.

"Oh, my order. Yes, of course. But you can call me Alonzo. My name is Alonzo, not 'Prease'," the woodchuck replied.

"Yah, Aronzo, what you want? I ret you see menu, maybe?"

Alonzo with no idea what this kindly old man was talking about, nodded and turned to look out the window. The cat was waving at him to hurry up. The woodchuck looked from the cat to the man and back again to the cat. Suddenly it was getting very warm and Alonzo was not so sure that he could do it. He again looked out of the window towards the car and Andre. The cat had his sunglasses off and he was gesturing wildly with both paws. Alonzo turned back to the man behind the counter and smiled.

"Who you rooking at, rittle boy? You want some spare libs? I take your order? You lead menu and you tell Hoy Toy what you need, yes?" he said in a very friendly tone.

Alonzo stood still. He was trying very hard to make the words come out, but there was no sound, not even a grunt. He looked back at the car. Andre was jumping up and down and pounding on the steering wheel with both paws. He turned to the old Chinese human creature and gave it one more try.

"Wood!" he whispered. "Wood!"

"Wood?" the old man whispered back.

Alonzo nodded. The old man stood up straight and scratched the top of his head. He looked down at the woodchuck again. "I be light back, don't you wooly, I be light back," he said as he turned and went through the doorway behind the counter. "I be light back!"

The woodchuck suddenly felt his tail starting to come out from under his shirt. He looked around.

70

No one was there. Quickly he reached back and tucked his tail back up, this time being very careful to wrap it tightly inside. Just as he finished, a little Chinese girl appeared from the side of the counter. She was wearing blue overalls and carrying a small ball on a white stick which she stuck in to her mouth. The little girl came right up to Alonzo and looked at him carefully. Alonzo still did not move.

The old man was now standing behind the counter. He leaned over and spoke: "I bling rittle person rike you. You tell granddaughter about what you rike."

Alonzo smiled and looked down. The little girl who had long black hair cut just above her eyes, walked around the little woodchuck and studied him carefully. She took the lollipop from her mouth and touched the top of the ski hat with her hand. Alonzo pulled his head to the other side and tried not to look at this curious human creature. She turned to the old man behind the counter. "This is one strange looking kid, grandfather," she said.

The old man looked down at his granddaughter and smiled. She was now walking behind the wood-chuck and looking at the back of his shirt. Alonzo hoped that she could not see his tail tucked up inside of it. He wondered why he had agreed to do this. He had had enough new adventures for one day. Alonzo

moved around to make the little girl's attempt to
study him more difficult. She put the lollipop into her
mouth and stepped closer to the counter. She looked
up at her grandfather, who was leaning over the
counter looking at the two of them. "Grandfather,
this kid looks
like a wood-
chuck with a
shirt and a ski
hat on!" she
exclaimed.

The old
man reached
down to touch
Alonzo on the
top of his
head. Suddenly the door burst open and in walked
Andre. "Well, is the order for Wood ready, or what?"
he demanded. The little girl's mouth opened and the
candy fell to the floor. She seemed to be frozen
against the front of the counter.

"What seems to be the problem? I mean, I send
my buddy, Al, in and you guys are what, giving him
some kind of hard time because he looks a little
weird, huh?" complained Andre. "There are other
Chinese restaurants you know! Come on Al, we're
outta here, man!"

"No, no! We velly, sorry, velly sorry. What you rike, what you rike?" the old man said apologetically.

Andre stepped up in front of the woodchuck and stood right next to the little girl. Looking at her sternly in the eye from behind his sunglasses, he said, "That's more like it. We have an order under the name of Wood, Wood." The little girl did not move.

The cat looked up at the old man who was now standing up straight behind the counter. "Ah, you have order. Yah, Wood. I be light back, light back," the old man asssured him. With that he again went through the doorway behind the counter.

Andre turned once again to the little girl. He adjusted his sunglasses and smiled a small smile at her. She closed her mouth and although she tried to speak, she could not. The cat then turned to Alonzo. "Do you still have the money I gave you, Al?"

The woodchuck nodded his head, reached out with his paw, and handed the cat the twenty dollar bill he had been holding. Andre took the money and eyeing the little girl said: "You got a problem, babe?"

The little girl shook her head. "Good!" said Andre. "By the way, you dropped this. I'd wash this off before putting it back in my mouth if I were you," the cat advised, as he picked up the lollipop and handed it to her "A 'thank you' might be nice, eh?"

he finished. The little girl wiped the tip of the lolli-pop with her hand and then she put the candy back into her mouth, still staring.

The old man reappeared with a brown bag and handed it to Andre. The cat smiled and handed the old man the twenty dollar bill that the woodchuck had crumpled and gotten all sweaty. "Ah, yes, that be ereven dorrar and ereven cents." he said as he took the bill from the cat's paw. "You rike exta fortune cookies?" he asked, handing a small bag to the cat, while he made change at the cash register.

"Yes, thank you," said the self-assured cat. "That is very nice of you and your lovely grandaughter."

"She vely rovery," the old man said, as he smiled at her. "She vely smart sometimes," he said with a big smile. "But not today. She think Aronzo a wood-chuck." He let out a big, huge, friendly laugh as he handed the cat his change. "Today, she vely funny!"

"Funny?" asked Andre, "No. Perhaps a bit strange though. Come on, Al, let's get out of here." The two animals turned and with the cat carrying the bag of food, they headed out the door to the parking lot. As they got into the car, Alonzo looked back. He gave the little girl a small wave and winked as the car pulled in front of the restaurant. The little girl did not move.

Chapter 10

An aroma of warm Chinese food filled the interior of the car. The two animal friends sat together in silence as the car approached the parking lot exit. Andre brought the car to a stop. He looked over at the woodchuck seated beside him. "Where to, little guy?" he asked.

Alonzo looked over at the cat with the hood of the sweatshirt pulled off the top of his head. "Ah, er, I don't know. I thought we were going back to the human burrow to eat this stuff," he answered.

"The human burrow? It's a house, man, a contemporary-styled house. My goodness." Andre told him. "If we go back there, the food will be cold and it won't taste as great as it smells," he added, taking in an extra big breath of air. "Let's just get something to drink with it and then eat it at the park." When the woodchuck said nothing, Andre took this to mean that it was okay with Alonzo to alter the original plan and go with his latest brainstorm. "The park will be fun. There are always lots of things to do there and lots of fun people," Andre said as he pulled the car out onto the street and headed further away from the human burrow and Alonzo's woods.

Alonzo spoke up after they had been driving for only a few minutes. "Thanks for helping me out in the Chinese food place, but I think that I could have done it. I just got a little sick to my stomach when the little girl started to look at me. I'm kind of tired and I think that going to the park or whatever might be a bit much for me and..."

"Nonsense!" Andre said, interrupting the timid woodchuck. "The day is still young. Besides," he went on, as he nervously looked about, "I think that I

turned the wrong way, so, ah, we can't go home right now. I mean, I know where we are and all, so, ah, we'll just go a different way. Yeah, we'll go this other way, and then we'll be there, like later."

Alonzo noted again that the cat did not have everything under control. It occurred to the woodchuck that the cat might even be lost. "Do you know where we are?" he wondered aloud, looking at Andre, who was still straining to recognize landmarks and street signs, as the car continued onward.

"Of course I do," the cat quickly responded. "But things look a lot different when you see them from the inside of the cat box instead of behind the wheel of a car."

The woodchuck began to get very upset. Unable to control himself, Alonzo began to cry. At first the tears just welled up inside of him and he rubbed his eyes as he looked away from Andre. But the more he thought about being so far from the woods and the things he knew best, the tears exploded through his paws and ran down his snout. He tried to sniffle them away, but there were too many. Then he began to shake. There was no hiding it now: Alonzo was crying hysterically.

Andre, concentrating on the road did not notice Alonzo at first. But as the little woodchuck started to sob and shake, Andre looked quickly over, then back to the road and finally back again. "Oh brother, this is just great," Andre blurted. "Just because I'm having a little, little problem here, you go all to pieces on me. Come on, come on. Relax. Has your old buddy ever let you down, huh?"

This just made the woodchuck cry even harder. "I'll never see the woods or my family again," Alonzo sobbed. "We're lost and it's all your fault," he added, without thinking of the tone of those last words.

"My fault? Now just a minute, buddy boy. I got you this far, didn't I? I mean, how many woodchucks do you know who go driving in cars or eat Chinese food or do the wonderful things that we've done today, huh?" the cat growled. "Now, you cut this foolishness out and get a grip on yourself. We'll get home, but first we are going to the park to enjoy this stuff," Andre said, nudging the bag with his paw.

"I'm not hungry. I just want to go home," the woodchuck sniffled.

"Look! I'll tell you what," the cat said in a calmer, more soothing tone, "I'll just ask someone the directions and then we'll enjoy the shrimp, the spare ribs, and the special veggie dish I got for you. O.K.?"

"And we will go right back home after that? You promise?" Alonzo asked.

"Yah sure, kid. We'll go back home after we go to the park." the cat said quickly.

"I don't want to go to the park. I want to go home," whined the woodchuck.

Andre looked at him and nodded his head slightly, while scouring the sides of the road for someone to ask directions.

Alonzo tried to get himself under control when

suddenly, he was thrown against the side of the car, bumping his head on the window. Andre pulled the car to the right and stopped right next to an old man, pipe in his mouth and cane by his side, who was sitting on a green bench at the side of the road. The cat pushed the button and the window came down as he shouted, "Hey, mister! Hey, bud! Do you know where this road goes, eh?" Alonzo ducked down in the seat as the cat leaned over to await the old man's response.

The old man very slowly reached up with one hand and took the pipe from his mouth. With his eyes squinted and his brow very wrinkled, he peered over at the cat. "Whad ya say, sonny?" he rasped.

"I said," Andre responded impatiently, "where does this road go?"

The old man put his pipe back in his mouth and scratched his snow white hair with his hand. He then looked down the road to the left, took the pipe from his mouth and looked down the road to the right. Then he looked at the cat with one paw on the steering wheel and the other on the window sill and said, "Why it don't go nowhere, it stays right here, ay yup."

Andre looked down at the woodchuck who had

stopped sobbing and was now showing the slightest hint of a smile. The cat looked over at the old man and again at Alonzo, nodding his head and laughing. "Ok, Ok, we are lost. We are definitely lost," he said.

The smile on Alonzo's face suddenly turned to a frown. He bit his lower lip to stop it from quivering, but it was no use. Again he began to cry.

Chapter 11

Andre sat back in his seat and looked out of the driver's side window. The Chinese food still had a wonderful smell to it, but the cat knew that it was getting cold. The little woodchuck was sitting next to him crying more than breathing and the old man on the green bench was adjusting the pipe in his mouth. The cat opened the door on his side and got out of the car. He walked around the front and stood in front of the old man. "Look, I'm lost," he whispered. "Just tell me how to get to Olde Farm Road and I'll get into my car and drive off. Now that's pretty simple, isn't it?" he added rudely.

"Nice car, sonny," the old man finally said, after an awfully long pause. "Is that yours?"

Alonzo had now raised himself up in the seat and was looking over the top of the door. Andre turned and looked at the car. "Yeah, it's my car. I mean I'm usin' it, obviously. Why?" the cat said in a mocking tone, responding to the old man's inquiry.

"Just curious," the old man replied. "I guess, nowadays, they'll give any fool a license."

Andre looked up into the sky and did the quick count to one hundred and forty by sevens. He looked at the old man again and said, "Olde Farm Road, do you know how to get there?"

"Maybe. You got a pencil and paper?" the old man said, reaching into his pocket for a match to re-light his pipe. He struck the match on one of the coarse boards on the bench and it burst into flame. He put the burning match to the top of his pipe and puffed a few times, blowing white smoke into the air. For a moment his entire face was hidden by the cloud of smoke he had created. Alonzo was fascinated by this fire-and-smoke breathing human creature and put his nose out of the window so he could get a better sniff.

Just as the smoke was rising above his face, the old man began to cough violently. He coughed and coughed until his red face became even redder. Alonzo's eyes widened. Andre, who had come back

to the car to search for a piece of paper and something
to write with, rushed back to the bench and began to
pound on the old man's back with one paw. When
that did not help, he pounded on his back with both
paws. The old man was leaning forward and gasping
for air. He took several deep breaths and sat up
straight. His face was almost purple and his eyes
were very watery. He held his arms up in the air and
let out a couple of little coughs. Then his color began
to get better and the old man looked at the cat and the
woodchuck and smiled. "Wow, that was a close
one," he whispered, gasping for air. "I can never
understand why I ever bother to light that foolish
thing. Thanks."

Andre got down off of the bench and stood again
in front of the old man. The old man was wiping his
face with a white-dotted red bandanna. Alonzo was
standing on the seat to get a better view of the old
man. The cat took a piece of paper and a pen from
the pocket of his sweatshirt. He looked up at the old
man and said, "Well, Olde Farm Road?"

The old man took a deep breath and looked at the
cat holding the pen and paper in his paw. He then
looked over at the woodchuck in the shirt and ski hat.
He shook his head. "My, my, they sure give strange

haircuts these days, don't they?" he said, nodding towards the woodchuck. Andre looked at Alonzo. "Let me see. Olde Farm Road? Olde Farm Road. Well," he thought out loud, "I think that if you go straight ahead about two miles and turn onto Pleasant Street and.....no, no. Maybe if you go up to the next light and take a left and then go to the school and take the third street after the variety store on the corner........."Andre stopped writing. "Oh, I know," the old man went on, looking at the cat and gesturing at him to write, "You turn around. Go about three blocks past the old firehouse and take that left, then you go four streets up and then, and then..." The old man sighed. He shook his head and looked up at the impatient cat who had again stopped writing. "Sonny, I just don't think that you can get there from here. Nope, you can't."

Andre just stood completely motionless in order to make sure that he had heard the words of the old man correctly. He dropped the pen and the paper to the ground and leaped at the old man, grabbing his shirt and shaking him back and forth. "What?!? What did you say?" he screamed at the defenseless old man. Now he was jumping up and down on the bench next to the old man and throwing his arms about wildly. "What do you mean that 'you can't get there from here'? What do you mean?"

Alonzo quickly got out of the car and rushed over to the bench, to protect the old man from Andre's outburst. The woodchuck put himself between the old man and the cat still jumping around on the bench and pulling at his own sweatshirt in frustration with his paws. The old man held his arms up to prevent the cat from striking him. Andre continued to jump about. Alonzo picked up the old man's cane and used it to keep the cat away from the two of them. The old man moved down the bench to put more distance between himself and the incensed cat.

"STOP IT!" Alonzo screamed as he held the cat at bay with the cane. "Calm down, for crying out loud. We can ask someone else. Let's get out of here."

Andre was beginning to tire and his energy level was no longer fueled by his anger. His jumping up and down began to decrease and, after a few little jumps and one tiny one, he sat down on the bench and buried his head in his paws. Alonzo gave his friend a gentle, consoling pat on the shoulder. The woodchuck looked up at the staring old man and handed him back his cane.

Alonzo, satisfied that the cat had calmed down,

sat there for a minute between the old man and the cat. Then he hopped down from the bench and opened the car door. There on the floor of the passenger side was the brown bag with the Chinese food which he grabbed and brought back to the bench. He put the bag next to Andre and climbed back up to where he had been sitting. The old man was looking over the woodchuck's shoulder as he opened the bag. The Chinese food smelled divine and it was still very warm. Looking first at the cat and then at the old man, Alonzo spoke, "Who wants a fried shrimp, eh?"

Chapter 12

The three of them, the cat in sunglasses and the red sweatshirt the woodchuck, with the shirt and ski hat, and the old man pipe out of his mouth, sat on the green bench and ate Chinese food. Alonzo and Andre ate all the spare ribs and fried shrimp, and the old man shared the veggie dish with Alonzo, who admitted that it was indeed tasty. In fact, after experiencing vegetables cooked in that manner, the woodchuck wondered if he would ever eat them right from the garden again. He wasn't sure that his mother would understand at all.

"So, boys," said the old man when they had finished and Andre had thrown the empty containers away. "Where are you off to?" Both Alonzo, who was still sitting next to the old man, and the cat, who was now standing in front of them, leaning against the car, looked at the old man with raised eyebrows. "Oh, yeah, I forgot. You guys are trying to find Olde Farm Road. That's right," he continued. He watched Andre carefully guarding against any sudden moves. "Now, if you wanted to, perhaps you could come with me and I could help you find that place," the old man suggested.

"Oh, I don't know about that, ..." said Alonzo very quickly as he glanced at the cat.

"Wait a minute," interrupted Andre, stepping forward and putting himself between the woodchuck and the old man. "Where are you going, huh?"

"I was waiting for the Belmont Street bus. I was going to go to the bowling alley and meet some friends. The bus is late," responded the old man. "Say, maybe you could give me a lift and I could ask one of my buddies how to get to Farm Avenue."

"Olde Farm Road. Olde Farm Road," Alonzo bellowed from behind Andre, who was thinking carefully about the old man's plan.

"Bowling, eh?" said Andre. "Well that's right up my alley, old man. Right up my alley, hah, hah. Get it, woodchuck, huh? Right up my alley," he screamed, laughing hysterically all by himself. Alonzo failed to understand the joke. The old man shook his head and looked up.

The cat stopped laughing. "Ok. Ok. Do you know how to get there? I mean, can you tell me what streets to take, huh?" he asked impatiently. The old man stared back at the cat and nodded. "Well, what are we waiting for? Let's get into our wheels and roll," said Andre, as he turned to open the door for the old man. "You can get in the back. I don't want Al sitting there in case he gets sick or something. I want him to be close to the window. Right, Al?"

The old man, with the help of his cane, got to his feet and shuffled over to the open door of the silver car. The cat pushed the lever to slide the front seat forward so that the old man could get in. When the old man reached the car, he put one hand on the roof to steady himself and the other hand he used for his cane to get in and to hold back the seat back before stepping in. He turned to Andre. "My name is Silas Daniels, but my friends call me Jack," he told the cat and the woodchuck, who was pushing him forward from behind.

"Well, Jack, I'm Andre and my friends call me Andre. This guy, this guy," the cat said, "his name is Al Wood and I have no idea what his friends call him, because I just met him today. I call him whatever the spirit moves me to call him at the moment. You know what I mean?" he added, winking at Jack and touching the old man on the side of his leg with his elbow.

"Alonzo! Alonzo Woodchu..." Alonzo blurted out before he felt a hard blow from the cat's fist in his belly. "Ow!"

"Sorry, kid," Andre said, helping the old man into the back seat. "It's Alonzo Wood." The cat nodded to the woodchuck, who acknowledged the correction slowly.

"Well, it is very nice to meet both of you. It really is. And if I haven't thanked you for the eats, please understand that I am truly grateful for your sharing them with me," said Jack, as he settled his old and tired body into the back of the car, behind the passenger seat. "You know, you see a lot of stuff on television these days that gives young people a bad reputation. You two guys are very kind."

"That's swell, Jack," said Andre, as he came around and got into the car behind the steering wheel. "Just get us the directions to where we want to go and you can put us in your will." The old man did not hear the smart remark of the cat as the sound of the engine starting muffled the words. The woodchuck liked the old man and was beginning to tire of Andre's occasional mean comments. The woodchuck looked into the back seat at the old man. They smiled at each other as the car pulled away from where it had been parked.

Chapter 13

"Ah, Jack, we've passed this shopping center twice now," said Andre, looking through the rear view mirror at the old man seated in the back seat. "I mean, do you know where you are going? This isn't one of these 'can't get there from here' deals, is it?"

The three of them had been riding around in circles for the better part of an hour. The old man, in response to the cat's query ,was looking out the window and furiously trying to recognize landmarks that would lead him to his final destination: the bowling alley. He rubbed his snow-white hair with his left hand and squinted as he peered again through the front glass of the automobile. Alonzo was intently watching his new friend and hoping that the old man would see something soon. The little woodchuck was beginning to sense that Andre had lost his patience with their new passenger. There had already been one skirmish and no one wanted another.

"Hold it, sonny," Jack said rather suddenly. "Over there. Take that turn over there, behind the gas station. There it is. See the bowling ball and the pins on the sign? Can you see it? Aw right," he said with great relief as he pointed out the window to the right. "I knew it. I just kept missing it. I reckon it's 'cause

I usually don't do the drivin' when I'm on the bus, you know."

"Right, Jack, right," said a relieved Andre as he put on his turn indicator and steered the car over toward the gas station. Alonzo looked too. He was not exactly sure what it was that he was supposed to see. What he found most unusual were the large numbers of yellow objects opening and closing their big red, green and quick yellow eyes. Alonzo thought that these things were very powerful and important. It seemed that all of the cars obeyed them when the yellow things slowly blinked their big red and green eyes.

If the truth were known, Alonzo had no idea what bowling was. As the woodchuck stared out the window, he saw a huge sign with a big black ball and some tall white sticks with red circles on them. It looked like the ball was smashing into the sticks and knocking them apart from their neatly arranged order. Under the sign, he saw a very big building.

"Look, Jack," said Andre, as he maneuvered the car through the parking area toward the front door of the bowling alley. "I'll drive up to the door and you can run in and get one of your friends to come out and give us directions from here to Olde Farm Road. Ok?" The old man, who seemed pleased that he had directed his new friends to the bowling alley, smiled

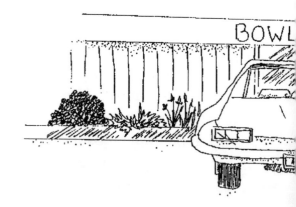

BOWL

in agreement with the cat.

Andre brought the car to a stop at the front door right under the big sign. The woodchuck looked up at it with his mouth wide open. "Hey, Al, ole bud, the back seat passenger can't get out unless you move your bod," said Andre, giving Alonzo a rather strange look. "I really don't want to sit here all day watching you admire the work of some moronic sign painter, eh kid?" The cat then gave Alonzo a shove.

"Er, ah, sorry," said the woodchuck, embarrassed. "I'll help you out, Jack. Just a second. Let me get the seat pulled forward." Alonzo finished, as he opened the door and looked for the little lever under the seat that would let the seatback move forward.

Jack smiled at the woodchuck in the ski hat and put his cane out onto the parking lot pavement as he

94

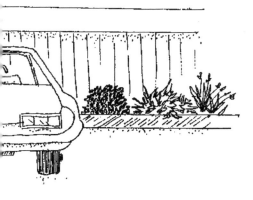

reached forward with his other hand to push the seat
and steady himself. He then put one foot out, pulled
himself up onto the front of the rear seat and began to
squeeze the rest of his tired old body out of the back
of the sleek silver car. Alonzo stepped back and
offered a paw to help the old man, who seemed to be
struggling. Jack took the woodchuck's paw in the
hand that was not holding the cane and finally eased
himself out onto the tarred parking lot. "Thanks,
pal," he said to Alonzo, patting him on the head, as
Jack limped by him toward the doorway.

"Hey man, don't forget. We came here to get
directions. Remember?" shouted Andre, as the old
man disappeared inside the bowling alley. "Get in
Al. We'll wait. I have a strange feeling about this."
Alonzo got back into the car with a very puzzled look

on his face. He was quite confident that Jack would come through and did not share the concern of the cat.

They waited in the car. Andre left the engine running and the radio was playing wonderful music that completely fascinated the woodchuck. Everything seemed so peaceful and pleasant.

Suddenly the door to the bowling alley swung open and Jack came hobbling out. He put his hands on the open window sill on Alonzo's side, bent down and looked in at the two animals. He seemed confused. "Hey fellas, what day is it today, huh? It is Wednesday, right?" the old man asked of them both.

Andre shook his head and then buried it down into his paws, which were gripping the top of the steering wheel. Alonzo raised his eyebrows, turned, and looked at the old man. The little woodchuck had no idea what day it was as woodchucks never really had any reason to consider such thoughts in the woods. One day was just like any other. Alonzo was beginning to learn that things outside of the woods were very involved indeed.

The cat looked up at the old man leaning in through the window. "It's Thursday, Jack. Thursday," Andre said quietly, as he glared at a confused Jack.

"Are you sure?" the old man asked in a raspy

voice, hoping that the cat was wrong.

"It's Thursday, Jack. T-H-U-R-S-D-A-Y," the cat said spelling it out. The old man stood up by the side of the car and began to rub his head with his right hand. With his left hand he steadied himself against the side of the car. He appeared to be thinking. "What difference does it make, Jack? Your friends can only give directions on Wednesdays? Is that it?" Andre sneered at him impatiently.

"They're not here," Jack whispered as he turned back and leaned inside the window.

"What did you say?" the cat responded, leaning over toward the old man.

"I said they are not here," Jack answered.

"What do you mean they're not here? I mean, you are sitting on the bench, waiting for the bus to take you to the bowling alley to meet your friends and they aren't here! Are you early?" demanded Andre.

"No," replied the old man looking down at his wrinkled, aged hands holding the window sill.

"Jack, the suspense is killing me," screamed the cat. "Where are your friends? What's going on?" The woodchuck, fearing the worst once again, tried to brace himself in case Andre made a leap at Jack. Alonzo put his paws in such a position that he hoped would fend off any impending attack by the half-crazed cat.

"I bowl with my friends on Wednesdays," Jack answered quietly again. "I don't know anyone here."

Alonzo looked over at Andre. The cat's eyes had widened. He was getting a look that Alonzo had seen just before he had grabbed the old man on the green bench. "This is some kind of old people's joke, right, Jack? Ha. Ha. Ha," laughed Andre, with an insane sound to his voice.

The old man looked at Andre and shook his head very slowly several times. Suddenly, Alonzo could feel the cat tense up and begin to prepare for action. Thinking as quickly as woodchucks can think, he opened the door and pushed the old man to the side. As he did that, Andre fell flat on his face, landing half in and half out of the car, thrashing wildly with his front paws. The cat's sunglasses fell to the edge of his nose. Andre looked up, glaring furiously at the woodchuck and the old man who were both standing at a safe distance.

"So, Jack," said Alonzo, taking the old man by the hand and heading for the door to the bowling alley, "care to smash some white sticks with red circles on them?" The two of them went inside and Andre was left pounding the pavement with both paws in utter frustration.

Chapter 14

The explosion of noise which greeted the little woodchuck and the old man as they entered the bowling alley was deafening, especially to Alonzo, who had very sensitive hearing. He clung tightly with his paw to Jack's wrinkled hand and drew himself closer to the old man's body. Alonzo was very glad that he had put on the ski hat tightly over his ears.

As the old man and the little woodchuck walked toward the main counter of the bowling alley, Alonzo was looking quickly about. He was certainly not prepared for what he heard and saw. It was a very brightly lit place with lots of different smells. His little nose was working overtime as he tried to figure out what the various odors were. Alonzo could smell the now familiar pizza, and smoke, which he had seen and smelled when Jack lit his pipe. Other aromas he sniffed for the very first time.

Jack was standing at a counter very much like the one at the Chinese restaurant. Alonzo stood very close to Jack. He was holding onto the old man's leg while peering around at the bowling alley. There were lots of human creatures standing or sitting by shiny wooden paths. At one end of each path he could see a brightly lit area containing the neatly stacked tall, thin, white sticks with red circles on them. The humans were rolling small black balls down the shiny wooden paths and knocking down the sticks. The woodchuck watched carefully. It seemed that when the human creatures knocked down almost all of the sticks, they were very happy and jumped about. Some of the humans would even clap their paws together. But if they knocked down one or two or none, then they had very sad faces. Alonzo noticed that some of them would laugh at the others when the black balls ran along the side of the shiny wooden paths without hitting any of the sticks. "Wasn't it much harder to send the ball down the path without hitting the sticks? Why were the human creatures were laughing?"

But, what really caught the interest of the little woodchuck was what happened when all the white sticks with the red circles were knocked down. A big fence came down from above the fallen white sticks and swept them away. Then more white sticks dropped from a brown thing and more new sticks waited to be knocked down again. Sometimes the humans would step on something and even if they had not knocked all of the sticks down, the fence would come and sweep the sticks away. It was clear

to Alonzo that the humans seemed to be enjoying watching each other and had fun seeing the white sticks fall.

"Hey Jack. Everyone missed you yesterday. Where were you, huh? Did you forget that Wednesday is bowling day with the guys?" asked the man standing behind the counter. Alonzo stared at the tall man with very short, tiny black hairs sticking out of his face. In his mouth he had a long brown stick with lots of big clouds of white smoke coming from it. The woodchuck turned his sensitive nose toward the rough looking man and sniffed at the smoke. It smelled terrible, nothing like the sweet smell from the old man's pipe.

Jack looked at the young man with the cigar in his mouth and smiled as he tried to avoid breathing the horrible smelling smoke. "Nah, Butch, I needed to take a rest, so I took yesterday off."

"Well, everyone was askin' for ya, but I figured somethin' like that was up," replied Butch, as he sprayed some shoes with a can of disinfectant and puffed on his big cigar. "So, is this that little grand-nephew of yours that you're always yappin' about, eh Jack?" The bowling alley manager now bent over the countertop to look at Alonzo, who was staring right back at him through the smoke. The woodchuck quickly looked away and grabbed the leg of the old man even tighter. "He is a bit weird lookin' though. I mean, no offense, Jack. It's just hard to see the family resemblance when they're that young. Must be from your wife's side, eh?" Butch said, reaching for some more shoes that were on the countertop and needed to be sprayed.

"Yeah, that's my grandnephew all right, from Ethel's family. Yep. He's come to try out bowlin' for the first time, Butch," said Jack proudly, patting Alonzo gently on the head. "He is a shy one though, huh? You got any open lanes we could use for a bit?"

"Sure Jack, let me check the board and see what we got," answered the bowling alley manager. He stepped away from the counter in front of the old man to check a big board with lots of switches and blinking red lights. "How about number forty on the end, Jack? Is that ok with you?" Butch called over. The old man nodded his approval. "I know you wear a size nine shoe, Jack. What about the kid? Ya gonna get shoes for 'im or ya gonna let him do it in his socks?"

Alonzo looked down at his hind paws. What was it with socks? The little woodchuck looked up from his feet at the old man, who was smiling down at him.

"I reckon the little fella can go in socks. He won't need shoes. Anyway, he's got real small feet and you probably don't have shoes that tiny," responded Jack as he took the size nine shoes and the paper score sheet from Butch. "Come on Al, we'll show you how to bowl. Ya know, knock down the white sticks with the red circles on them."

The old man put the shoes under one arm, took Alonzo's paw in his hand and walked over to alley number forty at the far end of the building. The little woodchuck tried not to look at any of the human creatures as he walked with his friend, but he felt that the human creatures were certainly looking at him. He was a little concerned that he would be discovered, that someone would recognize that he was not the old man's grandnephew.

Alonzo's thoughts were quickly interrupted by a loud commotion behind him at the main counter of the bowling alley. So they turned to see what was going on. "Oh my goodness!" groaned Jack. "Wait here, son. I got to go help our little buddy." Alonzo looked up and saw Andre at the counter in an argument with Butch, the bowling alley manager. The cat was waving his arms at the manager, whose face was completely engulfed in cigar smoke.

The old man turned to go back to the counter. Alonzo followed; in fact, he had never really let go of Jack's leg. So, as the old man hobbled toward the confrontation at the main counter of the bowling alley, he called as he struggled back to where Andre was: "Hey, fellas, take it easy. What seems to be the problem?"

Butch looked very upset and turned quickly to Jack. "This very rude kid says he's with you. Says you're gonna pay and wants to bowl without bowling shoes. I tell him he's gotta have 'em. But he claims he doesn't know what size he is and wants me to figure it out. I ain't runnin' no shoe store, Jack. You better teach this guy some manners besides bowlin', man. I suppose that he's related to ya too, huh?" The bowling alley manager and Andre were glaring at one another as Jack stood between them.

"Sorry, Butch. Calm down. Yeah, this kid's with me, too. I was wonderin' where he'd gone off to," said Jack, bending over and looking right at Andre. "He won't need shoes anyway. He's got socks on. See?" the old man said, pointing at the white hind paws of the cat.

Butch stared down at Andre's paws through the cloud of smoke from his cigar. Alonzo, with his mouth in its familiar open and surprised position, watched the bowling alley manager . "Oh, yeah. Sorry, Jack."

"Come on, boys. Let's do some 'serious bowlin'," said Jack, as he grabbed Andre hard by the hood of his sweatshirt and pulled him away from Butch's view. Then the old man, still with the wood-chuck attached to his leg, and the very annoyed cat who was still glaring at the bowling alley manager, headed for alley forty for what was, Alonzo hoped, some 'serious bowlin'.

Chapter 15

"You know, Jack, I was doing okay with that smoking baboon at the front desk. You didn't have to come to my rescue," complained Andre, as he was being forcefully escorted to lane forty.

"Sure, Andre, you had it well under control," said Jack calmly, without looking at the irate cat. "Probably given another minute, you would have been smoking that cigar, lit-end first, eh?" Alonzo laughed and quickly tried to muffle this behavior by putting one free paw over his mouth. With his other paws, he was tightly wrapped around Jack's leg.

Andre stole a quick, angry glance at the little woodchuck. "When I want your opinion, I'll ask for it," he mumbled to Alonzo.

"Boys, please, can't we just enjoy ourselves?" asked the old man as the trio arrived at their assigned lane. The two animals, the cat in the sweatshirt, which was still in the old man's grasp, and the little woodchuck in the shirt and ski hat, nodded. They walked around their bench and the old man let go of Andre's sweatshirt and sat down. Alonzo relaxed his grip on Jack's leg and let himself slide gently from his safe haven to the floor.

As Andre stood there surveying the scene and occasionally looking back in the direction of Butch, his nemesis, Alonzo stared at the long shiny alley stretched out before him. The woodchuck now barely noticed the intense sounds of bowling pins falling and balls crashing down the alleys, as he was fascinated by the shiny wooden path and the white sticks at the end. He turned around and watched as the old man slowly removed his sneakers to put on the bowling shoes.

At the very next alley, alley number thirty-nine, three small human creatures and a large female creature were very involved in bowling. At first they did not even notice the two strange creatures and the old man. But Alonzo looked at the humans. There were two little boys, a bit younger, he guessed, than the little girl in the Chinese restaurant, and a woman with a very small girl sitting on the woman's lap. It was the little girl with the thumb in her mouth who first noticed the strange little woodchuck. She removed her thumb and began to make little grunting noises, pulling on her mother's shirt, to get her attention. She pointed at the woodchuck and the cat in the sweatshirt, who was now sitting on the bench next to the old man and looking right at the little girl. The mother at first ignored the little girl and then quickly looked over at the two animals and the old man. She smiled and then went back to her intense concentration on the activities of the two little boys, so that the little girl made even louder noises as she pointed wildly at Andre and Alonzo. Again the woodchuck's feet were frozen to the floor. But the mother, without even looking again toward the animals, grabbed her daughter's hand, forcing the thumb back into the little girl's mouth, so as to stop any protests. However, the

little girl's eyes were still transfixed on the woodchuck and the cat.

Andre looked over at the little girl staring at him. Wanting to help Alonzo, Andre got up from the bench while Jack was bent over tying his bowling shoes and, never taking his eyes from the little girl, walked over and stood next to the scared woodchuck. The little girl watched the cat's every move. Andre nudged his friend in the direction of the bench and then performed a deep formal bow toward the little girl. Her eyes opened wildly and she began to struggle in her mother's arms, but the little girl's mother, without so much as a glance at Andre again put the little girl's thumb back in the little girl's mouth, tightening her grip on the squirming tot. Seeing this, Andre smiled, showing all of his teeth, then pushed the sunglasses down to the end of his nose and peered at the wide-eyed little girl over the top of the frames, causing the little girl's eyes to roll toward the back of her head as she passed out. Her mother, looking down at her daughter, seemed thankful that even with all of the noise in the bowling alley, she had finally fallen asleep.

Jack stood up from the bench and took a few steps in his bowling shoes to make sure that they gave him the proper feel. Satisfied that the shoes were going to do the trick, he shuffled over to the ball rack which stood about the same height as the woodchuck when he was standing on his hind legs. There were nine or ten balls on the rack. Some were all black and others were multi-colored: black with red, pink, or blue splashes of color on them. Jack looked down at the balls and picked up a multi-colored one. It fit in the palm of his hand. He swung his arm forward and backward as he turned to face the tall, slender white sticks standing proudly at the other end of the alley. He took a couple of steps and then slid on one foot as he let go of the ball which fell to the surface of the alley with a bang. The ball then rolled, at a fairly good speed, toward the candlepins at the end of the

alley. Alonzo stood up on the bench so he could get a better view. After the ball struck the pins, all but four of them fell down. Alonzo looked quickly at Jack who was moving his body in a strange way as if hoping that the bowling pins would see his movements and imitate them, thus causing them to fall. Despite the old man's wild gestures, the remaining pins stood perfectly still.

Jack went back to the ball rack and picked up one of the all-black balls. He stood at the head of the alley and seemed to be thinking about how and where to launch his next ball. After a brief moment he stepped back, swung his arm, took the two steps and slid, hurling the ball down the alley. Alonzo hopped a few times on the bench, thinking that this would give him a better view, as he followed the ball on its journey.

There were several bowling pins lying in the alley. The ball, which Jack had thrown, struck them and bounced to the side without touching the four standing pins. Jack stamped his foot on the floor and moved again from side to side. It made no difference. Alonzo was disappointed. Jack shook his head and went back to the ball rack for his third and final ball.

This time the ball knocked down one of the pins, leaving three. The old man seemed pleased. He turned and shouted at Andre, who was sitting on a chair with a pencil in his paw. "Give me seven, kid." Andre scratched a seven onto the score sheet just below Jack's name, which he had written along with his and the little woodchuck's.

As the machine lowered its fence to sweep away the pins and re-set new ones, Alonzo was very excited. He jumped down from the bench and headed for the ball rack, eager to try this new activity. He was intercepted by the cat, who got there first. "Wait a minute, Al," Andre said, holding back the woodchuck with one paw. "It's my turn. I go next. Read the score sheet," he continued as he pointed to the table where the old man was now seated. Alonzo looked over and bit his lower lip as Jack motioned to him that it was not his turn. Alonzo put his head down and slowly walked back to stand next to Jack.

Andre reached for a ball from the rack. As he did so, one of the little boys reached for the same ball. "Hands off, pal," the cat warned the startled little boy.

"Ah, em, huh? What?" said the little boy, leaving his mouth open.

"That's my ball, kid," Andre told him harshly. "Cat got your tongue?" he said again, taking great delight in the overused phrase. Quickly, the little boy turned to the woman for some answers, but she was busy admonishing the other little boy for sticking his gum under the bench. Andre smiled at the little boy and picked up the ball.

Now, because of his size and the size of the ball,

Andre could not hold it in one paw. He needed to use both paws and swing the ball between his legs to get it going down the alley. The cat stood at the very top of the alley and swung the ball back four times as he bent way over and launched the ball straight down the middle of the alley. It is a little known fact that most cats, certainly North American cats, are right handed. Andre was no exception. The ball, therefore, with this extra force from Andre's strong right hand, started down the middle of the alley and then made a very sharp turn to the left landing in the gutter where it continued its travel. The ball went right by all of the pins, hitting none of them.

"Wait a minute. I can't bowl here. The alley is warped. Is this some kind of a trick, Jack? Huh? I mean, did you and that goon up at the counter set me up?" bellowed Andre, obviously embarrassed by his gutterball. The little boy was still focused on the cat. "Hey, what are you looking at? I didn't see you do any better," said the cat rudely to the surprised child.

"Take your second shot, kid," Jack answered, ignoring the cat's claim of foul.

"All right, but this alley had better not be messed up or we're leaving," replied Andre. He took another ball and stood this time on the far right of the alley, almost against the wall. As he launched his second ball, it went down the alley along the right side. Andre turned and smiled at Jack and Alonzo. As the cat nodded his head, he noticed the woodchuck covering both of his eyes with his paws. Andre turned quickly and saw that the ball, almost at the pins, had made a sharp turn to the left and once again landed in the gutter, passing by all of the pins. The cat did not turn around, but walked over to the ball rack.

"This is your last ball, kid," the old man said, laughing at Andre's antics. "I thought you were a star at this, huh?"

"I just need to get warmed up. This is a practice turn, right?" asked Andre, without turning around.

"No, this counts," Jack told him, as he smiled at Alonzo. "Maybe you ought to try turning around and throwing the ball down backwards!"

Andre took another ball from the rack. He examined it closely and then handed it to the little boy, who was still standing in the same spot. "That ball has something wrong with it," the cat said to no one in particular. Andre then carefully selected a multi-colored ball and satisfied this was his best choice, he once again approached the alley.

This time he first stood on the far left. Then he moved to the middle. The cat stared at the pins at the end of the long alley. Andre acted like he could hear the pins teasing him about his two previous gutter balls as he stomped around the floor trying to get into position. "Come on. We don't have all day you know," called an impatient Jack.

"Yeah, I know," Andre answered. "I'm gonna try a new technique." The cat turned and faced the old man and the woodchuck. He bent over and looked down the alley backwards through his legs as he held the ball. He then swung his arms not three or four times, but six times and on the lucky seventh time, he exerted all of his strength. As the ball shot through his legs Andre became confused and forgot to let go.

The ball took off right down the center of the alley and the cat with it. He started to roll over and wrap around the multi-colored ball as it shot towards the pins standing at attention.

The old man dropped his pencil and gaped in amazement. Alonzo jumped to his feet and ran to the top of the alley. The little boy's mouth opened even wider. Then there was a tremendous crash of cat-fur and bowling ball as this duo collided headlong with the bowling pins at the end of the alley, knocking them all down.

"That's a ten!" shouted Jack, as he reached for the pencil.

Chapter 16

Alonzo was stunned as he stared down the alley at the fallen pins and the cat with the sweatshirt lying still on his back. The little woodchuck glanced quickly back at Jack, who was writing something and did not look up. Next to Alonzo was the little boy. He too, was transfixed by the sight of Andre lying among the pins at the back of the alley. Suddenly and without any warning the little boy bent forward and pushed the pin reset button on the ball rack.

The woodchuck looked at the boy who was laughing as he stepped away from the rack. The little boy had a wild and sinister look. Alonzo was horrified as he saw the fence come down and start to sweep the pins and his friend, Andre, into the back of the alley. "Jack! Jack, stop that thing. It's got Andre, Jack. Stop that thing!" the little woodchuck called to the old man.

It was too late. The old man, hearing the cries of Alonzo, got up from the table and shuffled as fast as he could to the ball rack. By that time, however, the fence had come completely down and swept all the pins and the prone cat into the darkness at the back of the alley. A new set of pins dropped. Andre was gone into the pin setting machine.

116

The old man and the little woodchuck were quite a sight as they looked in vain for some sign of Andre. Alonzo buried his head in Jack's leg. The old man patted his shoulder with his hand. Neither of them spoke. The ball that Andre had used on that last shot rolled up and out of the opening onto the ball rack. Alonzo looked up from Jack's leg and watched the ball move down the rack and stop as it bumped into the balls already lined up there. The little woodchuck took one more longing look down the alley. Then with both arms locked around the old man's leg, Alonzo again buried his face into the safety of the old man's trousers.

The old man also looked away from where the cat had last been seen to follow the ball as it came out onto the rack. Not knowing what to do or say, Jack looked over at the little boy. The little boy was smiling and pointing at the end of the alley where the cat had been.

"Momma. Momma, that kid went down the alley and he's gone. Momma, he's gone," called the little boy to the woman with the little girl on her lap. The woman quickly looked up in an effort to locate her other child. When she first heard the cry of her son, she thought that his little brother had somehow gone down the alley. She was relieved to see her other son sitting behind the bench playing with the old man's sneakers.

"That's nice," she said, very matter-of-factly. "Why don't you push the button on our alley and bowl again? Your brother does not want to bowl anymore. Come on now, because we have to leave pretty soon." The woman never looked carefully enough to see the old man and the woodchuck glaring at her older son. The little boy standing by the ball rack looked up at the old man and took a small step backward to be out of the old man's reach.

As Jack turned his head, the little boy, in one very quick movement, pushed the button and scurried back to the safety of his mother. Alonzo let go of Jack's leg and tried to reach out and grab the little boy as he reached for the button. But the little boy was much too quick even for a woodchuck. "Why, you little so and so," snarled Jack, showing anger for the first time. "What do you think you are doing?"

"I'll thank you not to talk to my son that way, you old goat," said the woman angrily to Jack as she stood up to protect the little boy who had come to stand by her side. "Who do you think you are any-way, picking on a five-year old child? I am going to report this to the management. Come on, boys, let's go to the front desk." The woman, still holding her daughter, now out of her fainting spell, took both little boys and dragged them away quickly.

"Ja, Jack!" cried Alonzo, who was now standing on alley forty watching the pins being reset on alley thirty-nine. "Look!" The old man turned and looked where the woodchuck was pointing. He could not believe what he saw.

The pin setting machine had just dropped ten more bowling pins or was it nine? As the fence moved back out of the way and the machine had fully risen, Alonzo and Jack saw the cat. There was Andre standing in the second row of pins at perfect attention, the hood of his sweatshirt was over his eyes and he was facing to the side. The machine stopped and the fence was now clear of the front of the pins. At

first, Jack and Alonzo did not say or do anything. Then without further hesitation, Alonzo ran across to help his friend.

Even before Alonzo arrived, Andre was starting to move. First he opened his eyes. He had no idea where he was, as all he could see was the inside of the red sweatshirt. He moved his arms and as he did the pins to either side of him fell. Andre then began to struggle with the hood of the sweatshirt and in doing so he wandered blindly about at the end of the alley knocking down all the rest of the pins. Finally, just as Alonzo arrived, Andre was able to get the hood of the sweatshirt opened so he could see. He pulled it open with such force that he fell backwards. Lying on the floor he opened his eyes and there was Alonzo with his face right over the cat's.

"Ever have one of those days, kid?" were the cat's first words to the little woodchuck. "Well, this has been a beauty, eh?"

"Oh, Andre, are you all right?" the concerned woodchuck asked.

"Yeah, I'm great. I really enjoyed the ride in the pin setting machine. I enjoyed it almost as much as the vacuum," said Andre, as he struggled to get to his feet. "How many did I get, huh?"

"Well," said Alonzo, "If you count the ten that you knocked down here, then I guess you got twenty altogether. Yeah, you got twenty. You win, Andre, you win."

"I told you I was a great bowler, didn't I, kid?" Andre answered as he stood up and surveyed the fallen pins in alley thirty-nine.

"Not so fast, Andre," commented Jack, who had shuffled down the alley to help the woodchuck with the fallen cat. "You got ten on forty. This is alley thirty-nine. Whatever you get here does not count."

"Just a technicality, Jack. Just a technicality," said the cat as he started up the alley to the benches, leaving the old man and the little woodchuck standing there. Andre turned and looked back for a moment. "It's still my turn, right?"

"It's your turn, all right! Your turn to leave!" boomed a big voice from behind a cloud of cigar smoke. "Jack, you take these little trouble makers and get out of here before I throw you out," said Butch, who was blocking Andre's way.

"That's the old man and his two weird friends who upset my children," called the woman from behind Butch."The nerve of them. They should be thrown out. Scaring little children like that."

"Take it easy, lady. I'll handle this," said Butch, exhaling a huge puff of thick, greyish-white cigar smoke. Quickly Andre grabbed Alonzo, who had come up to stand by his friend, and pulled the little woodchuck with him as the cat rocketed forward toward the exit. Seeing that Andre and Alonzo were making their getaway, Jack approached the burly bowling alley manager to draw his attention from the fleeing animals.

"Come on, kid. We are outta here," whispered Andre, right into Alonzo's ear. "The old man can handle things. Let's go."

"But, but, wha, what about Jack? We can't leave him here," pleaded Alonzo, as he and Andre headed for the door and the safety of the car in the parking lot.

"There's no time, Al. Jack can take care of himself. Look! He's stalling the big ape. Move it!" demanded Andre, pulling the woodchuck with a quick jerk, as Alonzo was turning to watch the old man and the bowling alley manager through the cloud of cigar smoke.

"Bye, Jack," Alonzo called to his new friend. "Thanks for everything." The little woodchuck waved his free paw in the direction of the smoke. Andre was pulling him with such force that his feet did not seem to be touching the floor. Tears rolled from Alonzo's eyes as they reached the door. He would certainly miss the old man.

As the door swung open, they could just barely hear the old man calling: "Good luck, fellas, and thanks for the ride." Andre let go of the woodchuck and dashed into the middle of the parking lot to look for the car. He forgot where he had parked it with the excitement of their escape. With Andre running furiously about, Alonzo lost sight of the cat.

The cat stopped to catch his breath and looked behind him. There was no sign of the woodchuck. The situation was too dangerous to retrace his steps to find Alonzo. It was getting late and he had to get the car back before his people discovered how he spent his time when they were not at home. Andre hated to abandon the little woodchuck who he had befriended, but he felt he had no choice. The cat's attention was now totally focused on finding the silver car.

Suddenly, after several anxious minutes, Andre saw the silver car. It was right where he had parked it. He ran to it and looked about hoping that the little woodchuck was nearby. Andre called, "Al! Hey, Woodie, over here." There was no response. The cat looked back toward the bowling alley, where the manager and the woman with the three children were coming out of the door. Andre could see them all surveying the parking lot looking for some sign of the two animals. Andre had to save himself and get the car back to the garage at the house. He ducked down so that the humans would not spot him. Once he reached the car, he went around to the driver's door and opened it, climbing in carefully. Andre closed the door very slowly, hoping that the humans would not hear it shut. With his head turned to look out of the window, he reached for the keys to start the car. Then there was a voice.

"You know, you should always lock your doors and take the keys with you. It's not a good idea to leave them like you did," said the smiling and very relieved Alonzo, who was seated in the passenger seat with his seatbelt on. He handed Andre the keys. The cat started the engine and backed the silver car out of the parking spot. "By the way, what kept you?"

Chapter 17

"What kept me? Is that what you wanted to know, Al?" asked Andre, as the steered the car through the parking lot toward the street. He looked over at the little woodchuck in the passenger seat. "My, my, we're getting rather bold as the day goes on, aren't we? I think that you owe me an apology for that remark. If I had not escaped when I did, perhaps old Butch and those wretched children would be having woodchuck stew for dinner. Our splitting up and getting to the car the way we did was a master stroke of genius. Yes, a stroke of genius."

"Oh, Andre, I am really sorry. You are right," said Alonzo, "but, I just have one question." The woodchuck turned to look out the window as Andre pulled the car into the street.

"Yes, what is it?" the cat asked impatiently as he straightened the wheel and headed down the busy street.

"Did you by chance find out how to get back to the house? You know to the old farm or whatever, huh?" wondered Alonzo in a very quiet voice. Andre looked again at the wide-eyed little woodchuck."I mean, the bowling was really nice and all and I am sure that when I tell my brothers and sisters, they are never going to believe what I did and it really has been a busy day and, and, and......" A big tear appeared, trickling down his face and his lower lip began to pucker. "Um, what I mean is, what I hope is, um, um, the woods, will I ever see them again?" He began to shake and he could no longer hold the tears back. Alonzo was again crying uncontrollably.

"Hey, kid, take it easy. Get a grip on yourself. Have I ever let you down, huh?" Andre reassured his little friend. "Really Woodie, the day is young yet and there are more things to do." The cat reached over and gave the woodchuck a gentle pat on the

shoulder. Alonzo turned toward the cat, and a huge flow of tears burst forth soaking the cat's paw. The little woodchuck tried to stop the tears by pulling the ski hat down over his eyes, shaking and sniffling.

Andre silently shook the tears from his paw. They were lost and it was getting late. He knew that he had to get the car back soon or his secret would be discovered. This was all the old man's fault.

The cat looked around. He didn't see any landmarks that were familiar. If he had ever been in this area before, he had only seen it from the travel box from which all he could see was sky and an occasional radio/TV tower or the car's digital radio dial. "Ah, Al, kid, I know that this may not be a good time and all, but could I ask you something that has been bothering me all day?" Andre inquired.

"What?" Alonzo choked out between sobs, without looking at the cat.

"Oh good. Now, I don't want you to be offended or anything. I mean I like you and I think that I could be best friends with someone sort of like you and....This is hard for me to say, kid," stammered Andre.

"What is it, Andre? What do you want to know?" Alonzo asked again. His crying was subsiding somewhat and he was now curious about this big question that the cat had. It is well known that cat's are very curious creatures. Woodchucks are equally curious, but because no one makes woodchuck food commercials for television this little known fact remains obscure.

"Nah, forget it," said Andre. "Why don't we look for someone to get directions from. I mean to reassure you that we are going in the right direction. That's what I mean." Alonzo was looking right at Andre.

"Well, what is it, huh?" the little woodchuck asked again. "What do you want to know?"

"Are you sure you don't mind my asking you this now?" hesitated Andre.

Alonzo pushed the ski hat back up onto the top of his head. He had almost stopped crying, although a few small tears lingered at the edge of each eye. He wiped them away with his paw and said, "I won't know if I mind until you ask it."

"Well, you have a point there," the cat answered. "It's just that I really don't want to offend you. I mean you are upset and well, it's kind of a dumb question. Perhaps, I should just ask at another time; when you are feeling better."

This merely excited the woodchuck. Suddenly, he forgot about the woods. He forgot about the warmth of his nice burrow. He forgot about the fact that they were probably hopelessly lost. Alonzo was being driven on a new quest. He had to know what Andre was so afraid to ask about. What could it be, that it had bothered him all day? Alonzo looked himself over. He hoped that he did not have one of those prickly burrs stuck to his fur. He couldn't see anything unusual on his body other than the shirt, however. Maybe there was something on his face. Oh, how he wished that he had looked more carefully at himself in the refrigerator door back at the human's burrow. He touched his face quickly. Andre glanced over at the strange woodchuck.

"Woodie, are you all right?" Andre said with a great deal of concern.

Alonzo could barely contain himself. "Yes, yes, I am fine. What is it?"

"What's what?" the cat asked.

"What is the thing that has been bothering you all day?" Alonzo practically screamed, he was so excited. He reached over and pulled at the sleeve of the cat's red sweatshirt, saying, "Please, it's ok."

"Yeah, ok, if you insist," Andre said as he slowed the car under one of those yellow things with the red, yellow and green eyes. "Like, ah, how much wood, huh?"

"Would what?" the very puzzled woodchuck asked.

"Aw, come on. You're just afraid to say. You

know trees... wood. How much?" the cat replied as he looked up at the yellow thing with only its red eye open.

"Trees. Wood. What are you talking about?" responded Alonzo, now more curious than ever.

"Hey everyone knows, but they just don't know how much? I figured that you could tell me and then I would really know something. You know what I mean?" said the confident cat. The yellow thing closed its red eye and opened its green one. Andre hesitated for a moment as he looked at the strange woodchuck. The sound of horns beeping broke the silence. Andre turned his attention to the road ahead and the car moved forward.

"Know what?" the woodchuck finally asked.

"I mean if this is upsetting to you just stop me, ok?" the cat said. Alonzo took a deep breath, raised his eyebrows and nodded. Andre smiled and then revealed what had been troubling him all day: "How much wood can a woodchuck chuck, if a woodchuck could chuck wood?"

Alonzo sat in utter silence. His face was expressionless. Andre felt terrible for asking such a question. The woodchuck looked at the cat. "Probably as many pickled peppers as Peter Piper picked." he said calmly.

"Oh, of course. I knew that," the cat replied.

Chapter 18

It had been a remarkable day so far for both
Alonzo Woodchuck and Andre. As they rode along
in the silver car, each was thinking about what had
happened to them and how they had become good
friends. Alonzo smiled at the cat, who was concentrating on finding a landmark to guide him home.
Andre sensed that the woodchuck was watching him
and he looked back at Alonzo. Their eyes met and
they both laughed out loud. They were indeed
friends.

Alonzo looked around. He knew that he would
not be much help in finding the way back, but he
enjoyed all of the new sights that this day had brought
to him. The little woodchuck did notice, that there
were fewer yellow things with multi-colored eyes in
the sky and that the buildings along the side of the
road were no longer big with lots of cars parked near
them. The road was getting narrower and now he
could see lots of human burrows.

"Hey, Al," Andre cried out without warning.
"Look over there. In the park. What do you think
they are doing, huh?" Alonzo looked in the direction
that the cat was pointing. It was a large park sur-
rounded by a chain-link fence. Inside the fence were

probably fifteen little humans. They were wearing hats and some, the ones standing spread out in the park, had one huge hand. One of the little humans had a long stick in his hand and he was swinging it wildly around. Andre slowed the car and pulled next to the fence so that the two animals could watch.

Andre smiled and said, "I bet that this is another new one on you, eh? Well?" The cat looked over at Alonzo, rather surprised that the woodchuck did not have his mouth hanging open. In fact Andre was more confused. The cat scratched his head and then again spoke. "Stumped, Al? It is a bit....."

"Wow, oh my!" interrupted Alonzo. "Those humans are playing baseball. I can't believe it. The stories my parents told me are true. They are playing baseball." The woodchuck was so excited. He turned to the surprised cat, "Hey, Andre," he continued, "do you want to go over there? I mean, do we have time? Do you think that they would let us play? Well, what do you

132

think, huh? Andre? Andre? Are you listening?"

As the little woodchuck was reaching for the door to join the humans playing in the park, the cat could not move. Alonzo opened the door and tried to get out. The seatbelt was still on and as he swung his little body to the side to climb down, the belt tightened and he was suspended between the seat and the door about a foot above the pavement. Without thinking the cat reached over and pushed the orange button where the belt fastens and Alonzo dropped to the ground with a small thud.

"Ow!" the little woodchuck cried as his rear end struck the ground. He sat there for an instant and then quickly got to his feet. "So are ya comin'? Let's play some ball!" Alonzo pounded both of his hands together as though he were pounding a ball into an imaginary mitt.

"Hold on. Where do you think that you are going?" said Andre, as he tried to exhibit some control. "We can't be doing this. I have to find out how to get home and get this car back into the garage before the humans catch on to me."

"But, we can play for just a few minutes and maybe one of those little humans can give us directions," responded Alonzo. "Where is your sense of adventure? Or are you not very good at baseball? That's it isn't it, Andre? You can bowl and skate, but you can't play baseball and you don't want me to show you up, huh?" The little woodchuck was standing outside of the car now with both paws on his hips and feeling very smug.

"Oh really, Al. I am a natural. I can play ball with the best of them. Andre knows bowling. Andre knows skating and most of all, Andre knows baseball," the cat insisted. "It's you who I am worried about. What do you know about baseball anyway?"

"What do I know about baseball? Is that the question?" demanded Alonzo. "Who do you think invented baseball, huh?"

"Some very confused human, I would imagine." replied Andre, as he adjusted his sunglasses and pulled the hood of his sweatshirt off of his head. "Some human who enjoys boring other humans; that's who."

"Yeah, just as I thought. You don't know anything. I mean you're all caught up in woodchucks

134

chucking wood and you really never gave any thought to what great things my ancestors have done," Alonzo asserted. "Baseball was invented by woodchucks, Andre. A human stole the idea from us and now everyone thinks that that's how it all began. Woodchucks invented baseball." Alonzo looked over to where the human children were playing and nodded.

"Gimmee a break, Al," Andre said, laughing at this latest outburst from his friend. "How come you never told me this before? Get in the car and you can tell me this wonderous tale. If you went over there those kids might figure out you're a woodchuck. I mean no offense. Maybe you were there to steal baseball back, right?" Andre was now laughing uncontrollably. Alonzo turned from watching the humans in the park and glared at the cat.

"Very funny, Andre. Very funny," Alonzo complained as he climbed back into the passenger seat of the silver car. He closed the door and turned to the cat who was turning red from laughing so hard. "Abner Doubleday stole baseball from the woodchucks."

"Come on, man. I got to give it to you though. You have a wonderful sense of humor, Alonzo. No kidding," Andre said between bellows of laughter. Alonzo was not laughing. He looked right at Andre, waiting for this rude cat to get a grip on himself. It took him awhile, but finally, Andre stopped laughing and opened his tear-filled eyes. "Why, you're really serious about this, aren't you?"

"I am," answered Alonzo. "I mean, it's bad enough that these humans have taken baseball and made it seem as though they thought it up. Now, my friend, in whom I have put my trust, doubts me." The little woodchuck turned from the cat and stared straight out the front windshield. The two animals said nothing for a minute.

"Okay, I am listening. Let's hear it," Andre said finally, breaking a rather uneasy silence. "Tell me all about baseball. I really want to know."

Alonzo looked over at the cat and then looked out the window at the children playing in the park. He began to speak: "A very long, long, time ago, my ancestors, the Great Canadian woodchucks moved from the Lake Muskoka region of northern Ontario to the lakes region in New York state. The Great Canadians were a hearty, fun-loving group of woodchucks who were especially fond of group games. After a hard day in the fields avoiding angry farmers, they loved to relax and enjoy a competitive game of any kind. Even though they might have been tired, they were never too tired to engage in the excitement of a good game."

Alonzo looked over at Andre. He continued: "My mother has often told me that in those early days in Ontario, one of the favorite games was Capture the Flag. But as the woods were cleared for the farms, it was no longer the popular game it had once been. My great, great, great, great uncle, Ty Corn O'Cobb would spend the late hours of each night thinking about a game that could be played in the cleared land of the farms. Uncle Ty, who earned his name from his fondness for the Indian corn grown in those cold fields of Ontario, journeyed with the rest of his family in the late fall of 1838 to New York. He slept through the winter of '38 into the spring of '39. All during his winter sleep he dreamed of a new game that he and his fellow Woodchuckians could play on the farms where they now resided. The upstate region of New York was particularly beautiful with rolling hills and lush valleys crisscrossed by gurgling brooks and streams. Deep in the valleys, near the many lakes that covered the region were huge farms that supplied the food for the big city far to the south.

"Uncle Ty's family settled in a little town right on a lake. Their burrow was right plunk in the middle of a farm belonging to Abner Doubleday's family. There were several other woodchuck families living on this farm and they would often get together with Uncle Ty's family for after work recreation. It was

during one of these get togethers that Uncle Ty told
the others about the dream he had had during his
winter sleep. At first the older woodchucks had their
doubts about the logic of this new idea for a game and
they scoffed and laughed at the younger woodchucks
who wanted to give it a try. Uncle Ty was not dis-
couraged, however, and with his good friend Babe
Woodchuck, he tried to convince the others how
much fun a game like he had dreamed could be.

"The burrow where Uncle Ty lived would be the
home base for the game. The idea of the game was to
make a long journey without stopping. If you made
the journey without stopping, he called it a homerun.
Woodchucks, by nature, when they are hard at work
in the fields and gardens stealing vegetables from the
farmers move very slowly, but when they become
involved in serious games, then they run.

"But Uncle
Ty knew that
not all of his
friends would
be able to run
all that way,
around a whole
field. So he
decided that you
could make

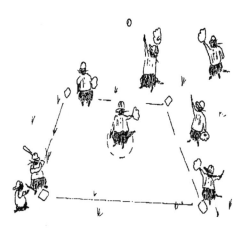

138

three stops and he named the stops: first base, second base and of course, third base. When he first told the others about this game there was much confusion. Often more than one woodchuck would stop at a base. Uncle Ty and the Babe would get upset and yell at all but one of the woodchucks at each base that they were out. Pretty soon it was necessary to have woodchucks stationed at each base to supervise the travels of the woodchuck runners. In fact, due to the heavy travel between second and third base, they put in a short stop in case anyone needed to rest or needed directions."

Andre was listening intently as the woodchuck continued. So far, he found the explanation to be rather convincing. Alonzo paused for a moment and went on: "Now at this point, I have to tell you that woodchucks are very social animals. We easily make friends with other creatures and they all seem to be fond of us. When my ancestors lived in Ontario, we became very close to a rather large beaver colony. The beavers were forever bringing us gifts as tokens of their appreciation for the work we would do in the gardens and fields gathering vegetables. Before he left for New York, Uncle Ty was given a beautiful, long wooden stick by Louis Ville Beaver. It was to be used for protection in the new land. But New York was a very friendly place, so Uncle Ty just put the stick in the back of the burrow until he came up with a use for it.

"Now the other myth about woodchucks is what you were talking about earlier, Andre. You know, 'how much wood can a woodchuck chuck'."

"I didn't mean to upset you. It was just a saying. I mean..." added Andre quickly.

"I understand. I am used to hearing ignorant stuff like that about woodchucks," interrupted Alonzo. "Let me go on. Woodchucks don't really chuck wood. What we do is chuck things at the wood. What I mean is that Uncle Ty finally found a use for the beautiful stick that Louis Ville had given him. Babe had the idea of chucking a stone at Ty and then when Ty hit the stone that the Babe had chucked, he would begin his journey to home base by running towards the first stop. It was great fun for Ty, but the Babe had to chase the stone and then he would run after Ty trying to tag him before he got to home. After a few days of this, the Babe sat down with Uncle Ty and told him that he needed to have help. Beyond the place where they had the stops, first, second, and third, were three big fields. Now Uncle Ty and the Babe wanted to keep it all very simple and they could tell that it was getting complicated, so they named the fields left field, center field and right field. The Babe got some of his friends to stand out there and look very bored until the stone came. Then they would pick it up and chuck it to the Babe. Back then the Babe had three of his closest friends to be the fielders, as Uncle Ty called this motley crew. In left field was Ted Woodchuck, a long, lean, splendid animal. In center field was Willie Woodchuck, who loved to catch the stone over his shoulder with his back to the Babe. Finally in right field was Reggie Woodchuck, who for some reason never really came into his own until the fall, around October.

"While all of this is going on, Abner Doubleday, who rarely did what his parents told him to do, would steal away from his chores at the farmhouse and hide behind a big rock or tree to watch Uncle Ty and the Babe. Abner would spy on them and make notes with his pencil and notepad. On one particularly hot summer's evening, Abner had an early supper and instead of checking on the cows in the barn as his father had asked him to do, he took a ball he had gotten from the general store in town and went to find a good hiding place to watch the woodchucks. On his way toward the fields he tripped over his boot lace and the ball he had been carrying fell out of his hand and rolled quickly down the path and onto the field. It was rolling pretty fast at that point and a young, fat little woodchuck, named Yogi, who was standing behind home base, caught it. The Babe saw this out of the corner of his eye as he was getting ready to chuck a stone to a new woodchuck who had joined them. 'Hey Yogi,' the Babe yelled, 'what did you catch?' When Yogi showed the Babe what he had caught, all of the other woodchucks laughed. From then on Yogi was known as the catcher."

Andre's eyes rolled up to the top of his head. Alonzo smiled at Andre and laughed. Andre laughed too. "Hey Andre, do you want to know how dugouts became known as dugouts?" asked the little woodchuck.

"Nah, that's okay. We have got to find out how to get to Olde Farm Road and it's getting late," he answered. The cat started the engine and pulled away from the fence next to the park where the children were playing baseball. Alonzo was watching them. Andre shook his head in disbelief. "Nah, that baseball story is preposterous," he thought. Alonzo turned toward Andre and winked at him.

Chapter 19

The silver car was moving slowly through the
streets as Andre searched for landmarks, now too
stubborn to stop and ask for directions. Alonzo was
enjoying the ride and found the sights to be fascinat-
ing. After a while, Alono began to tire and felt that a
nap would certainly help refresh him. He had been
through a lot already and he had a strange feeling that
there was more excitement to come.

Andre knew that he had made a wrong turn earlier as nothing looked familiar. If he retraced his
route, even though the old man had confused him, he
felt that he could get back on the right roads. Andre
glanced over at the little woodchuck seated next to
him in the car. Alonzo was sound asleep and his head
was nodding back and forth. Now Andre could con-
centrate on the task of driving. It was getting late and
panic over being discovered was starting to consume
the cat. His nine lives were wearing thin.

It is a known fact that cats love to dirty their
paws and walk about the family automobile leaving
little paw prints all over the hood and roof of the car.
Most cats do this because their owners fail to understand that cats don't like to remain at home all the
time. So,when a cat walks through the garden and
happens to get his feet all muddy, there is method in

his madness. He is preparing for payback time. If he can't be treated on an equal footing with a dog, then as a protest of sort, he'll annoy his owners with a few steps of the ole soft paws across the hood of that nicely waxed automobile.

Given that Andre used the car, he was less inclined to want to dance upon its hood. He was careful to keep a watchful eye on the hood though, to make sure that none of his other protesting relatives ruined the good thing that he had going. It was at a stoplight that Andre took one of those instinctive looks at the hood. Suddenly, Andre's heart skipped a beat. He looked again at the hood and his heart pounded in his little body: Dum, de, dum, dum. The light turned green and the cars behind began to honk their horns. Windows were rolled down and very unpleasant language was directed at Andre, whose eyes were transfixed not on little paw prints, but on a huge dent in the hood that most assuredly had not been there when they had left the garage earlier that day.

It was several moments before Andre collected himself enough to pull the car to the side of the road so that the irrate motorists behind him could get by. Some very uncat-like words were exchanged as the other drivers brought their cars around the silver car with the dent in the hood. Under most circumstances, Andre would have had a few choice words for them, but now he was focused on the damage to the car. He took off his sunglasses and looked out the windshield hoping that his vision had somehow been obscured but it was not an optical illusion. There was a very real dent there.

Up ahead there was a gas station and a place to park the car. He drove the few hundred feet and parked away from where he might be seen. Andre got out of the car and walked around to the front end. He was able to put his paw on the hood and feel the dent. He felt sick. The passenger door of the car opened and Alonzo got out. "Hey Andre, what are we doing here?" the little woodchuck asked innocently. "Did you get directions? Are we almost back at the house?

Huh? Andre? Gee, you don't look so good. Are you okay? What's going on?"

Andre looked at his friend and pointed slowly to the hood of the car. At first, Alonzo had no idea what it was the cat was pointing to. But then, even the inexperienced woodchuck saw what had upset the cat. "What are you gonna do, Andre? How are you going to explain this one?" the woodchuck wondered.

Andre turned and stared at Alonzo. "What do you mean 'what am I going to do?'" he bellowed. "This is all your fault!" Alonzo was dumb-founded. He let his bottom lip quiver and then his mouth fell open.

"My fault?" he said quietly. "What do you mean, my fault?"

"Oh, never mind. We have got to get this thing fixed or I might as well consider a change of breed operation. I wonder what I would be like as a porcupine?" Andre groaned.

"I don't know," commented Alonzo under his breath, "but, you would make a lovely rat." Andre turned slowly toward the woodchuck.

"What did you say?"

"Nothing. I didn't say a thing. I, I was thinking about what we should do and how this happened. Maybe someone hit it with a bat. That's what I said," Alonzo blurted out, thankful that bat and rat rhymed.

146

"Oh!" said Andre as he opened the passenger door and reached into the glove box in front of the passenger seat. "We'll call the insurance company and tell them just that. We'll tell them that someone hit the car with a bat and we have to have it fixed right away."

"What's a surance company?" Alonzo asked as he joined the cat.

"Not surance. Insurance. Insurance. What they do is take your money, a lot of it, and if something happens and your car needs to be fixed, they fight with you and pay for some of it," Andre explained.

"Why do they fight with you if you give them the money?" Alonzo wondered aloud to the cat.

"Because they think that it's fun and that you enjoy it as much as they do. I mean, it's bad enough that your car is all crashed up and you feel really bad about that, and then along comes the insurance company and they want you to remember how fortunate it is that they are there and all, so, they fight with you, so you don't forget," said Andre with authority. "They want you to feel that you are in good hands with them and that like a good neighbor they will be there."

"To fight with you?" Alonzo said with his eyebrows raised. "That idea sounds like someone with a piece of a rock for a brain."

"Exactly," Andre said as he pulled the papers in the glove compartment out and put them on the seat so he could examine them more carefully. "Ah, here it is. Freedom Mutual Insurance Company property damage hot line. All I have to do is call this number and they can tell me everything I need to know."

"Will they know how to get to Olde Farm Road or will you have to fight with them to find out?" Alonzo shouted to Andre as he hurried toward the tele- phone booth at the corner of the ga- rage. Soon he realized that he had a problem. Phone booths were made for tall people and even little kids could not reach the phone, let alone the dial pad. He turned and looked at the confused wood- chuck standing by the car.

"Hey Al, over

here. I need your strong shoulders," yelled the cat. He waddled over to the booth and looked up at the cat. "Do you want to do something really important?" Andre asked.

"Sure," said Alonzo, only too eager to assist.

"Good. Stand in there and I'll get up on your shoulders so I can make the call," said Andre, as he positioned the woodchuck just under the receiver. Then the cat climbed up on the woodchuck who really was taken by surprise. The ski hat he was wearing completely covered his eyes. Once Andre was standing firmly on the woodchuck's shoulders, he reached into the pocket of his sweatshirt and took out a quarter which he dropped into the phone. He then proceeded to dial the number.

Andre had the phone pressed up against his ear. After two rings a pleasant voice said, "Freedom Mutual Insurance Company, Beth Del Rufo,Technical Claims Specialist, speaking. What do you want?"

Chapter 20

"What do I want?" Andre asked.

"Yeah, what do you want? I am very busy. I have a lot of files on my desk, so just tell me what your problem is," Miss Del Rufo said in a very annoyed tone.

"Oh, I didn't know you were busy," the cat replied as he shifted his position on Alonzo Woodchuck's shoulders. The woodchuck was beginning to feel the weight of the cat and was having trouble standing still in the phone booth. In fact, he began to sway a bit from side to side. Andre was trying to balance himself and talk to the insurance company lady at the same time. "Anyway, my name is Andre Katz, K-A-T-Z, and I have a little problem with my car, er, ah, my friend's car that he, ah, let me use. Yeah, that he let me use and I......"

"So whad ya do, huh? Smash it up?" whined the insurance lady. "Now I suppose ya want me to get it fixed before ya give it back, right?"

Andre thought for a second and shifted his weight to prevent himself from falling off Alonzo. As the cat moved, Alonzo had an urgent need to scratch his nose, which by this time was also covered by the ski hat. The woodchuck let go of one of Andre's legs so that he could lift up the ski hat. Immediately, Andre lost his balance and fell backwards landing on top of Alonzo, who let out a huge groan as the cat came crashing down. Andre lost his grip on the phone. The receiver slammed into the side of the booth and swung wildly from its cord over the sprawled animals.

"Hey, what's going on?" said the voice on the other end, as the phone twirled about. "Hello? Hello?"

Andre struggled to his feet and standing on Alonzo's belly reached up and grabbed the phone. "Nothing is going on," he said breathlessly. "Look, Miss Roof...."

"Miss Del Rufo,Technical Claims Specialist!"

"Okay, Miss Del Rufo," the cat continued. "I really need to get this taken care of as soon as possible. The hood of my car has a dent in it and you have no idea how much trouble I'm in."

"I am not a body shop repairman, Mr. Katz," she answered. "Bring the car over to the company drive-in claim service and I will look at it and give you an estimate on the repair. Then you can take it to a repair shop and get an estimate and then we get to fight over the amount. But not today. I don't feel feisty enough. Look, why don't you bring the car over tomorrow."

"Lady, I have to have this car back today and fixed," Andre screamed into the phone, as he jumped up and down in frustration on Alonzo's stomach and chest. The woodchuck could do nothing but grunt and groan. Alonzo tried to get up, but the door of the phone booth was partially open and he was trapped. "I am coming over there now!"

"Now?" Miss Del Rufo said impatiently. "You are coming here now?"

"Yeah, now!" Andre said with authority. "How do I get there?"

"You can't get here from there," she said. Then Andre heard a click. Miss Del Rufo, the insurance lady, the Technical Claims Specialist, from Freedom Mutual Insurance Company, had hung up on him. Andre stared at the phone and then looked down at Alonzo, who was lying on his back.

"Get up, Al," Andre demanded. "We have to find out where this insurance company is so that I can give that woman a piece of my mind."

"I can't get up," Alonzo grunted.

"Why not?"

"It could be that you are standing on me, possibly?"

"Oh, yeah, I'm sorry," Andre responded as he stepped out the door of the phone booth so that the little woodchuck could get to his feet. Andre went back into the phone booth to look up the address of the Freedom Mutual Insurance Company. "Now let me see," Andre said, as he thumbed through the telephone directory. "How do you spell 'Freedom Mutual Insurance Company', hmmm?"

Alonzo was sitting outside of the booth and trying to straighten out his shirt and ski hat which was in a state of disarray.

Andre's head was buried in the book. "Yeah, and let's see. The drive-in-claims service," he said as he read down the columns in the directory.

"D-R-I-V-E," spelled out Alonzo. Andre turned toward the woodchuck on the pavement outside the phone booth. Alonzo had his back to the cat and was staring at a rather large sign across the street.

"What did you say?" the cat asked as he stepped from the booth and walked in front of Alonzo. Andre stood with his paws on his hips and was right in Alonzo Woodchuck's face.

"If you could stand slightly to the side, please,

then I could read the rest of the letters," Alonzo answered and he put up his right paw and directed Andre's attention to the sign across from the parking lot of the gas station. Andre looked and a big smile came across his face. There, across from where they were was the drive-in-claims service of the Freedom Mutual Insurance Company.

"Now won't Miss Del Rufo be pleased to see us," laughed Andre, as he headed for the car.

"She will?" asked Alonzo, as he got up to follow his friend.

"Most definitely. Most definitely, indeed," the cat answered.

Chapter 21

With the cat driving, they crossed the street to a very large, red- brick building with brown tinted windows. At the side of the building there was a large parking lot. Andre saw a sign with an arrow that pointed the way to the drive-in claim service area. He steered the car in that direction and pulled into the parking space.

As he opened the door, Andre checked the sideview mirror. His sunglasses were planted firmly on his nose and his sweatshirt hood was drawn tight, covering his ears. The cat winked at the woodchuck and walked to the door of the insurance company. At the door there was another sign: 'Please ring the bell for service.' Andre pushed the bell button and waited. No one came to the door. He pushed the button again and as he did so, he looked back at Alonzo and waved. Again no one came to the door.

Andre was starting to become very impatient. He pushed the sunglasses off of his nose, pressed his face up against the glass door and peered in. There, no more than a few feet inside the door, was a desk piled with files. In the middle of the desk was a small sign that said: 'Beth Del Rufo, Technical Claims Specialist'. Immediately behind the sign sat a woman with frizzy, mousey-brown hair. Arms folded, she stared back at Andre. The cat pushed the bell two or three times. Beth Del Rufo did not move, but grinned at the outraged cat. Seeing this Andre pounded his paws on the door and screamed at the technical claims specialist: "Lady, open this door! Open it! Open it now!"

"Say please," was the muffled response. Andre's eyes were wild.

"Okay, okay, please open the door, please?" the cat begged. Beth Del Rufo shook her head and grinned. She unfolded her arms and pointed to the clock on the wall, over her head, just behind her desk. The clock read: 4:25. Then she got up from her desk and walked towards the door where Andre was frantically pleading with her. Beth Del Rufo did not open the door, instead she pointed to another sign. The words were painted on the glass: 'Office hours: 9 am to 4:30 pm M-F'.

Andre looked into the office past the smiling

Beth Del Rufo. The clock on the wall behind her desk read 4:26.

Andre glared up at the lady standing behind the

closed, glass door. She lifted her eyebrows, shrugged her shoulders, turned and went back to her desk. As she sat down, she folded her arms once again and looked up at the clock. It read 4:27. Although he could not hear her through the glass door, Andre was able to read her lips: "Have a nice day, Mr. Katz. See you tomorrow." The cat nodded and then did a deep bow, after which he turned and got back into the silver car with the dent in the hood.

"Well, what's the story?" asked a curious Alonzo. "Are they going to fix the car? Did you find out how to get to Olde Farm Road? Andre? Are you all right?"

"Never been better, Al. Never been better," said Andre as he started the engine. Alonzo looked at Andre. The cat had taken off his sunglasses and pulled the hood of the sweatshirt off of his head. His eyes were fixed on the door to the office. The clock read 4:28. Andre revved the engine and it made a huge growling noise. "Hang on Al, we're gonna give Beth Del Rufo a real close view of that dent on the hood."

The noise of the engine startled the grinning insurance adjuster. She looked out and saw the ma-niacal look on the face of Andre. The car rolled back a few feet from the doorway and the sound became more intense. Beth Del Rufo suddenly felt very uncomfortable. Panic gripped her. The clock read 4:29. The car seemed poised to rocket forward. Then without any further hesitation, she leaped from her desk and grabbed the plumbers plunger she kept by her desk for such emergencies. She scrambled to the door and opened it as she waved her arms, signaling to the crazed cat. "Hold it! Just a minute. I can fix this in a jiffy and you won't even have to fill out the forms in triplicate in black ink or anything. Please!" she screamed. "There is still time." The clock read 4:30, but the terrified claims specialist was not even looking. Her eyes were transfixed on the silver car ready to leap forward with a vengeance.

Alonzo had both paws over his eyes when he heard the pleas of Beth Del Rufo as she bolted out of

the door carrying some strange stick with something attached to it. The woodchuck lifted his left paw to take a peek. When he saw what was happening, he glanced over at Andre. The cat was gripping the wheel and staring straight ahead. His paw was pushing the gas pedal down and letting it up in rapid succesion. Suddenly, Andre smiled and looked over at his friend. "Well, isn't that a sight. Seems our little friend wants to be helpful after all," he said.

Beth Del Rufo was pushing the plunger down onto the dent on the hood, working as speedily as she could without taking her eyes off of the cat sitting behind the wheel of the menacing silver car. "I'll have this fixed in a jiffy, sir. It will be just like new. There will be no charge and I'll even forget about the overtime too," she pleaded. The clock read 4:31.

Andre rolled down the window and jokingly called out to the very frazzled young woman, "Ah, could you check the oil and water while you're at it?"

"Oh, certainly sir," Beth Del Rufo responded without hesitation. "Yes, sir."

The technical claims specialist worked quickly with the plunger. Andre watched carefully and occasionally gave the engine a little gas. Whenever he did, she would jump back and shake from fear, which delighted Andre. Alonzo now had both eyes uncovered and watched, not really knowing what to expect next. Beth Del Rufo pushed the plunger down onto the dent one final time and suddenly there was a tiny ping of metal and the dent was gone. Andre leaned over the wheel and smiled at the spot where the dent had been. Beth Del Rufo backed way from the car, perspiration pouring down her face. She took a deep breath and looked skyward for a moment. Then she put the plunger to her lips and gave it a kiss.

"Rather than check the oil and water," asked Andre, "could you just give us directions to Olde Farm Road?"

"With pleasure. No problem, sir. No problem," Beth Del Rufo responded. Andre turned to Alonzo and winked. Alonzo smiled back.

The technical claims specialist went into her office and took a map from the top drawer of her desk. She made a few notes on a pad of paper and went out to give them to Andre. The cat examined them, thanked her, and gave her a little wave as the silver car without the dent pulled out of the parking lot heading for Olde Farm Road. Alonzo waved and watched as Beth Del Rufo continued to wipe her face dry.

Chapter 22

The ride home was uneventful. Andre recognized landmarks when they were halfway there. As they approached the driveway, the cat reached over and hit the button for the electric garage door opener and the safety of the garage appeared before them. They both let out a collective sigh of relief. Andre led Alonzo into the house and helped him get off his shirt and ski hat. Alonzo then tried to assist Andre with the sweatshirt, but because the sunglasses were stuck in the hood, it was almost impossible. The woodchuck pulled and the cat pushed. Andre could not see and as he lost his balance, he crashed into the side of the couch head first, then the two of them rolled about the family room. At first Alonzo laughed. Then he realized that something was wrong.

"Andre? Andre, are you okay?" The little woodchuck tried frantically to remove the sweatshirt from his fallen friend. Andre did not move. He just groaned.

"Andre! Andre, wake up. Come on, snap out of it. What's that noise?" demanded Alonzo, who was shaking the limp cat. "Get a grip on yourself. What is going on? What is that loud humming noise, huh? I'm scared." Alonzo finally succeeded in removing the sweatshirt from his friend's head. Andre groaned

again and rolled over. Both of his paws were covering his face as though he was protecting himself from
some impending disaster. He opened one eye and
stared at the little woodchuck who stood over him.

"Al, is that you? Are you okay?" the cat wondered as he tried to overcome his confusion. "I mean,
you're not hurt, are you? Wow, what a crash, eh? I
guess they won't mess with me again, and they'll
stay open until 4:30, for sure."

"What are you talking about?" the woodchuck
demanded. "Wake up, Andre. What is that sound?"

"Huh? What sound? Where are we?" Andre
asked, still unable to understand the nature of his
surroundings. The cat opened both eyes and suddenly
realized that he was in the family room in his house.
The sound of the electric garage door opening startled
him. "Yikes! I must have passed out. The people
who live here are home. They are coming, Al. Gee,
ya gotta get outta here before they see you. Hurry!"

Andre leaped to his feet and promptly tripped
over the red sweatshirt and fell flat on his face.
Alonzo stood there, frozen again. The cat quickly
untangled himself from the sweatshirt. He grabbed
the little woodchuck by the paw and led him to the
bathroom and through the open window to the back
yard. Alonzo climbed out and turned to his new
friend. "I had a wonderful time. Thanks for every-

thing. We'll have to do this again sometime, real soon, okay? May be we could play baseball or something, ya know?" With those words, the little woodchuck turned and scurried across the back lawn, past the garden to the safety of the woods.

Andre stood on the window sill at the open window and watched Alonzo. His brain was still a bit fuzzy. Suddenly the door from the garage opened. Andre dropped to all four paws. The family had returned. Andre meowed a greeting as the two boys and their parents entered together.

"Andre! Did you miss us, huh?" the two boys said almost as one when they saw the cat on the windowsill. The cat meowed in response and let them rub him behind his ears. Jonathan picked Andre up and gave him a gentle hug and handed him to Michael, his brother. Their father came into the small bathroom having heard their conversation with the cat.

"Hi, Andre. Hey guys, who left the window open? Has that been open all day?" the father asked. "Someone could get into the house and Andre could have gotten out. Let's try to remember to check things like that in the future, please."

Just then Jonathan and Michael's mother called to them from the family room area. "Why are these clothes down here? Jonathan this is your red sweatshirt and T-shirt. Michael, is this your ski hat? Let's go, guys, try to be more responsible, please. Certainly the cat hasn't been using this stuff." The two boys looked at each other. Michael looked down at Andre who seemed to be watching something outside through the window that their father was slowly closing.

"Hey, Dad, look at that animal out by the garden, at the edge of the woods. What is that, huh?" asked Jonathan. Andre struggled from Michael's arms and jumped to get a better look. "Look, he's standing on his hind legs and looking right at us. What is it?"

"It's one of those pesky woodchucks that just loves to eat the vegetables from our garden," said their father as they all watched the little brown animal. "Come on boys, you heard your mother, pick up that stuff and let's get everything put away."

"But, Dad!" protested Michael as he and his brother Jonathan left the small bathroom and went into the family room. The father stood at the window with Andre who was still sitting and staring out at the woodchuck.

"Now who could have put that stuff there, huh Andy?" the father said as he rubbed the back of the cat's head. "Perhaps you and that woodchuck were playing this afternoon, eh?" The father laughed and looked at the cat. Andre blinked his eyes at the man standing over him and looked back out the window. Alonzo Woodchuck gave Andre a barely visible wave with his paw. The father briefly stared at Andre and gently shook his head slowly as he turned away and went to join the rest of his family.

THE END